D0175135

SECRETS OF THE TERRA-COTTA SOLDIER

SECRETS OF THE TERRA-COTTA SOLDIER

YING CHANG COMPESTINE

VINSON COMPESTINE

AMULET BOOKS
NEW YORK

PUBLISHER'S NOTE: This is a work of fiction. Names, characters, places, and incidents are either the product of the author's imagination or are used fictitiously, and any resemblance to actual persons, living or dead, business establishments, events, or locales is entirely coincidental.

The quotation on page vii from *The Art of War* appears in *The First Emperor of China: The Greatest Archeological Find of Our Time* by Arthur Cotterell (New York: Holt, Rinehart, and Winston, 1981), page 44.

Library of Congress Cataloging-in-Publication Data

Compestine, Ying Chang.
Secrets of the terra-cotta soldier / by Ying Chang Compestine and Vinson Compestine.
pages cm
Summary: Through the stories of a terra-cotta soldier who has survived through the centuries, thirteen-year-old Ming, a village boy in 1970s China, learns the history of Emperor Qin, known both for building the Great Wall of China and for burying scholars alive, and how and why the terra-cotta soldiers came to be.
ISBN 978-1-4197-0540-3
[1. China—Antiquities—Fiction. 2. Qin shi huang, Emperor of China, 259–210 B.C.—Fiction. 3. Kings, queens, rulers, etc.—Fiction. 4. China—History—Qin dynasty, 221–207 B.C.—Fiction. 5. China—History—1949–1976—Fiction.]
I. Compestine, Vinson. II. Title.
PZ7.C73615Se 2013
[Fic]—dc23
2013006284

Illustration credits can be found on page 223.
Drawing of terra-cotta soldier by Jonathan Bartlett
Book design by Maria T. Middleton

Printed and bound in U.S.A.
10 9 8 7 6 5 4 3 2 1

115 West 18th Street
New York, NY 10011
www.abramsbooks.com

To Emperor Qin,

for commissioning a timeless mystery

When Emperor Ch'u fought against the Ch'in [Qin], one of his officers was unable to control his ardor before battle. He advanced alone, against direct orders, taking a pair of enemy heads. After praising his bravery and granting him an immortal existence as a terra-cotta soldier, the Ch'u general ordered the officer's execution, stating: "I am confident he is an officer of ability, but he is disobedient."

—Sun Tzu, *The Art of War*, ca. 200 BCE

CONTENTS

I

"WE FOUND AN EARTH GOD!"

MING FISHED OUT THE DREGS OF HIS BUCKWHEAT noodles with his chopsticks. He paused for a moment, grimaced, and then slurped them down. Now that the government was threatening to close the village's archaeological office, his father, bā ba, 爸爸, could soon be out of a job. Three days from now would mark the second year since the office had opened. But without an important discovery, the office would be shut down, marking the end of his bā ba's livelihood. After that, Ming would be lucky to have even plain noodles to eat for breakfast.

He set the chipped wooden bowl on the desk and picked up his English textbook. He stared intently at the strange letters. Since his bā ba's early-morning departure, he hadn't been able to focus on his homework. It had taken him an hour to meticulously line up the cryptic letters that resembled dead ants into just two short sentences: *Chairman Mao are bright sun. He leader we to a happy life*. Pages of dead ants were still waiting to be arranged.

Ming sighed and leaned back, balancing his chair on two legs and holding the flimsy textbook in his hand. On the cover, a worker with arms as thick as hams raised his hand, smiling broadly. Next to him was a peasant woman with round cheeks as red as fresh chili peppers. Below them were revolutionary slogans. Ming wondered if he could toss the textbook through the small door of the bucket-shaped coal stove across the room.

"Anyone home?"

The harsh voice from the courtyard startled Ming. He almost toppled over backward. He set the textbook down and ran outside.

Three grimy farmers stood beside a wheelbarrow under the hawthorn tree in the center of the yard. The

A communist propaganda poster similar to the cover art on Ming's textbook.

first signs of spring had appeared, and the branches were tinged with new, tender buds that hadn't been there a week ago.

Despite the early March chill, streams of sweat drew tracks down the farmers' dusty faces. They were out of breath and loudly sucking in mouthfuls of the crisp air. The eldest of them leaned against the tree for support.

Ming knew these frequent visitors well. The Gee brothers were always claiming they'd found something valuable and demanding money in return. Months ago, the fourth and youngest Gee brother had vanished. Some said he had committed suicide, while others insisted that he had run off after digging up an ancient treasure. Soon after his disappearance, the villagers began referring to the remaining Gees as the oldest, the middle, and the youngest—as if the fourth brother had never existed.

"What did you find?" Ming's stern voice belied his young age. He slowly descended the steps into the courtyard. His skinny frame looked even smaller next to the broad-shouldered, solidly built farmers.

The oldest Gee brother wiped his muddy hands on his cotton jacket. Ming noticed the mismatched buttons.

"Where's Old Chen?" the man asked gruffly. The frost

of his breath swirled in the air. His dark-skinned face was wrinkled like a dried peach. "We found an earth god!"

Ming backed up two steps of the stoop, putting himself at eye level with the farmers. He had long ago learned that looking up at an adult placed him in a weaker position. "My father is in Xi'an attending an important meeting," he said calmly. "He should be back later today."

Ming worked to keep his voice steady, trying to appear confident. He wasn't about to tell them that his bā ba, who appraised and bought artifacts for the museum, had gone to the city in a desperate and probably futile attempt to plead with officials to keep his office open.

The youngest Gee cursed loudly. "Turtle turds! We were counting on making some quick money." He had the same sharp chin and sour disposition as his older brothers.

Ming was irritated by the Gee brothers' greed, but his curiosity got the best of him. It was unusual for the farmers to bring anything big enough to require a wheelbarrow. He stepped down to take a look.

The youngest Gee quickly moved in front of him, blocking his view. "Now, hold on. What about our payment?" He thrust out his hand.

Ming sighed in exasperation. "You'll have to wait until my father gets home."

Every time the Gee brothers brought in discoveries, Ming's bā ba told them that he would pay them in two days, after he had had a chance to assess the value. Yet every time, they demanded the money on the spot.

"What did you find?" Ming asked, silently cursing himself for showing interest.

"Something very valuable!" declared the middle brother, the one with the bald head.

Ming's bā ba had taught him that buying artifacts

Just as the Gee brothers would have done, Chinese villagers worked in the fields, maintained roads, and performed other menial tasks. This villager wears typical clothing of the era.

from farmers like the Gee brothers was like bargaining for vegetables at the market. Once the seller knew you wanted them, he would insist on an outrageous amount of money.

"Where did you find it?" Ming asked.

"We were digging a well on the east side of the village and struck something hard about ten feet down." The oldest brother jerked his thumb over his shoulder. "I'm telling you, this one is worth a fortune! And we want our money now!" His sharp, beady eyes challenged Ming.

Suddenly, blossoming anger replaced Ming's seed of curiosity. Most of the farmers in the village were reasonable, but the Gee brothers always looked for soft persimmons to crush. Instead of lowering his eyes, as was traditionally expected when a youth talked to an elder, Ming matched the old man's gaze.

"If you don't want to wait for my father to appraise it, just take it to the Xi'an museum yourselves. But make up your mind! I have to go to school soon." He wished he didn't have to deal with the Gee brothers all by himself.

"We can't push this old wheelbarrow twenty-two miles!" protested the oldest brother.

"All right," said the middle brother sullenly. "We'll wait. But we want to get paid as soon as Old Chen gets home!"

Weary indifference drifted over Ming. "Bring it into the house, and I'll give you a receipt."

As the men pushed the wheelbarrow up the stone steps, grunting with exertion, Ming glanced inside it. He struggled to conceal his excitement: A life-size clay torso lay among a scattering of bronze arrowheads and disembodied clay limbs. Next to one of the legs was a clay head. The young-looking face bore an expression that was blank yet somehow arrogant. The high cheekbones and thin nose made it seem distinctly refined. Atop its meticulously sculpted hair sat a small round hat.

It was the most fascinating artifact Ming had ever seen, and by far the largest. Would this discovery help his bā ba convince the government to start some serious archaeological excavations in the village? Ming wished he had a way to contact him, but the only phone in the village was at the Political Officer's home. And he wasn't about to let that man know of his bā ba's absence.

Once inside the house, Ming picked up the head. He assumed the same critical expression he used when bargaining for cabbage. As his fingers brushed a grainy square at the back of the head, a sudden warmth radiated from it into his hands and then through his body. Ming turned the head over and studied the character inscribed on it: field, tián, 田.

"Hey! Be careful with the earth god!" the oldest brother shouted.

2
THE TERRA-COTTA HEAD

THE GEE BROTHERS UNLOADED THE BROKEN TERRA-cotta statue in the workshop, which also served as kitchen and living space for Ming and his bā ba.

A plastic clothesline stretched across the room. It sagged under the weight of the damp green garments that hung over the stove. Along one wall were shelves heaped high with basins, bowls, and books. A desk stood against the opposite wall.

Ming brushed transistor tubes and various electronic parts to one side of the desk and carefully set the head down. He picked up a worn stub of pencil and a pad of paper with the big bold heading XI'AN ARCHAEOLOGICAL INSTITUTE, 1958–1974. After clearing his throat, he delivered the instructions he had dictated many times since he had turned thirteen, a year ago.

"Please write down your name and address so my father can contact you. You will be compensated if your discovery is valuable." Even though Ming already had the Gee brothers' information, he wanted to maintain the formality of the transaction.

"Of course it's valuable! You tell Old Chen it's worth at least fifty bags of rice!" As the youngest brother snatched the pad and pencil from Ming, his broad shoulders knocked loose one of the shirts hanging from the clothesline. It fell to the ground with a *plop*.

None of the brothers bothered to pick it up.

"Hey, I just washed that!" Ming protested.

"Oh, look, he can do women's work!" the middle Gee brother sneered.

The three men chuckled.

Bristling, Ming angrily pushed aside the youngest brother, who was laboriously writing on the paper. Ming picked up the shirt and tossed it back over the line.

The youngest Gee threw the pencil and paper onto the desk. His hand paused in midair, then reached for a red pin with Chairman Mao's profile. Below Mao were gold characters proclaiming "Serve the People," wèi rén mín fú wù, 为人民服务. The pin was a rare edition Ming's bā ba had brought home from Xi'an.

A highly sought-after pin featuring the profile of Chairman Mao.

Eyes flaring with anger, Ming quickly grabbed it and swept it into the desk drawer.

Deprived of the pin, the youngest brother clenched

his hand into a fist. "Don't try to cheat us!" he snarled. "We'll be back for our money!" As he stormed out, his feet pounded the floor with enough force to kick up chunks of dirt. His brothers followed, muttering in agreement.

Ming closed the door behind them, relieved to shut out both their grating voices and the chilly early-spring air. He took a few deep breaths to gather his thoughts and then walked into the back room, which served as storage space as well as the bedroom. The government had built it onto the back of the house when Ming's bā ba became the museum's representative. Along with the addition, they had given him an official document, declaring that anything unearthed in the village was the property of the Xi'an museum.

Ming filled a small bamboo basket with egg-size pieces of coal and returned to the front room. He tossed a few of them onto the low-burning fire, then fanned the flames. After setting an aging kettle on the stove, he sat down near the desk, gazing curiously at the broken soldier. Where did it come from? Could it be from a tomb? Would it be enough to convince the government to keep the office open and resume paying his bā ba's salary?

Ming had prayed to gods known and unknown, to

ancestors named and unnamed, and even to Chairman Mao that his bā ba would make an incredible discovery that could lift them out of this backward village. How he missed the movie theaters in the city. And the indoor bathrooms—they were warm even during the worst snowstorms! More than anything, Ming missed his friends in Xi'an. Ever since he and his bā ba had arrived in the village of Red Star, the kids had treated him with a hostility he did not understand. He often wondered if it was because he was from the city and represented a world they didn't know.

Ming spotted a small square piece from the military chess game that he and his bā ba liked to play. He picked up the rough, handmade tile from under the desk and tossed it into the desk drawer, smiling. He had memorized the wood-grain pattern on the back of his bā ba's important pieces. Ming had learned that if he could find his bā ba's general and assassinate it with one of his precious bombs, he was guaranteed victory. But last night, Bā ba had removed both generals from the field, smiling knowingly at Ming. "The generals need some rest. The colonels will lead the battle tonight."

Somehow, Ming had still managed to win the game. This morning, before departing, his bā ba had patted Ming on the shoulder and said, "The colonel will be in charge in the general's absence."

Ming glanced at the clay head—and froze. Had the nose just twitched? It couldn't have! He leaned closer, staring intently.

This time, the eyes seemed to follow him.

Impossible! Ming shook his head, annoyed at himself for entertaining such silly thoughts. He reached over and picked up a bronze arrowhead from the floor, rubbing off the dirt with his thumb and forefinger. The edge pressed into his skin, still razor-sharp beneath the grime.

Maybe he should sell the arrowheads as scrap metal for food, like other village boys. If he was lucky, he might even get enough money to buy two hard-boiled eggs. He quickly shook off the idea, imagining his bā ba's disapproving look.

Ming gazed outside, where the sun was peeking out from behind fast-moving clouds. He felt as if someone was staring at him. He quickly looked around the room. Again he caught sight of the head. He could have sworn that the eyes blinked and the ears wiggled, but when he turned on the plastic desk lamp, the head bore the same blank expression as before.

An unearthed terra-cotta head.

Ming shook his head in exasperation and wondered if the changing light from outside was playing tricks on him. He picked up the head and held it under the bulb, squinting at the 田 character inscribed on the nape of its neck. Could it be someone's name?

"Hello, young man! Are you going to assemble me?"

With a loud yelp, Ming dropped the head and jumped back, pressing himself against the wall.

The head landed face-first on the desk with a dull *thunk.*

Ming stared at it with a mix of terror and fascination. It slowly rolled sideways, until one ear rested on the desk and the other faced up.

"Hey! I'm delicate! How would you like it if I tossed

your head around?" The head raised its eyebrows in mock curiosity. The gravelly voice took on a commanding tone. "Clumsy boy, come over here and put me upright!"

Ming glanced at the door behind him.

"Come on. I won't bite!"

Ming was rooted to the spot, as stiff as a frozen fish.

"If you help me," the head coaxed, "I shall tell you some exciting stories about me and my friends—and maybe even a few secrets about the tomb we live in. Does that sound like a fair deal?"

Hesitantly, Ming crept forward. He gingerly righted the clay head.

"Much better! Now, sit down," the head ordered.

Ming pulled up a wicker chair with a shaking hand and plopped down.

3
GETTING ACQUAINTED

"H-H-HOW CAN YOU T-T-TALK?" MING STAMMERED.

"Don't be afraid. I know how you feel." The terra-cotta head's now flat and unhurried voice made him sound like one of the old men at the teahouse about to tell a suspenseful tale.

"How could you know how I feel? You're—you're made of clay," Ming protested, trying to smooth the fear out of his voice.

"I used to be a human like you, though not as thin and

brittle." The head paused and sniffed derisively. "As you can see, I was better built."

"Better built? I bet if *you* had grown up on nothing but buckwheat noodles and old cabbage, you'd have turned out differently," Ming replied bitterly.

The head glanced at the chipped bowl sitting on the end of the desk. A few strands of thin noodles clung wetly to the edge.

"Is that what you are eating? Hmmph. My mother cooked the best noodles! That is probably why I was much taller and stronger than the other boys my age."

Ming wanted to say that his mother used to cook him all kinds of delicious food, but the head didn't give him a chance.

"I heard those men call you Ming. My parents named me Stone, Shí, 石!"

"They called you Stone? Why not Mud?"

Shí gazed balefully at Ming. "Don't you know that unattractive names were given to children so ghosts would not steal them? Besides, my name was prophetic. Here I am, strong as a rock!" The head wiggled from side to side.

Shí's sarcasm and good-natured taunts reminded Ming of his friends in Xi'an.

"You must have a pretty generous definition of 'strong.'" Ming tilted his head at the broken terra-cotta pieces.

Shí grinned. "I'd like to see how you would look after being buried for two thousand years!"

"Two thousand years!" Ming's face lit up with excitement. "What were you doing down there all that time?"

"I'm a brave soldier in the army that protects Emperor Qin Shi Huang's mausoleum!" Shí grinned proudly.

"Army? How many of you are there?" Ming's heart pounded.

"Thousands! But I can't tell you the exact number," Shí said guardedly.

"My bā ba was a history professor. He knows all of Emperor Qin Shi Huang's secrets!" Ming retorted.

"What's a professor?"

"A teacher. He used to teach at the best university in Xi'an."

"Xi'an? Where is that?"

"Do you know of Xi'anyang?"

"Of course! That's where Emperor Qin's capital was."

"Well, they call it Xi'an now."

"Hmm . . . that's far away. How did you end up here?"

"It's a long story." Ming sighed. "Our leader, Chairman

Emperor Qin took the throne in 246 BCE, at the age of thirteen. He ruled until his death in 210 BCE, at the age of forty-nine.

Mao, favors the peasants and workers who supported him, but he dislikes the educated men and women—the 'intellectuals.' My bā ba wasn't very enthusiastic about Mao's policies, so the government sent our family here to be 're-educated' by peasants."

"Emperor Qin did not trust scholars, either!"

"I've read that he burned some of them to death." Ming picked up a book from a stack on the desk. "My bā ba has a lot of books on Emperor Qin, and I have read them all. I know exactly how Qin became the first Emperor of China, Zhōng Gúo, 中国." He held the book up in front of the head. "It's all in here!"

Shí stared blankly at the brown cover.

"Wait . . . can you read?" Ming asked suspiciously, pointing at the characters *History of Qin,* Qín Shi, 秦史.

"Reading and writing is for scholars and merchants." Shí sounded embarrassed. He paused and said haughtily, "I doubt that book can tell you the whole story, as I can. I was there! You may be smart, but apparently not smart enough to keep from interrupting me."

"Sorry! Please go on." Ming leaned back in his chair, grinning with excitement.

4
SCHOOL

PRIOR TO THE QIN DYNASTY, CHINA WAS DIVIDED into seven warring states that constantly fought one another. Emperor Qin conquered and unified China in eight years. But soon a new enemy emerged.

One day when I came home from gathering wood, I found my mother weeping and my father squatting next to the stove. When he saw me, Father led me into the court-yard, away from my mother.

"I have been drafted to work on the Emperor's Great

Wall, Cháng Chéng, 长城. You are fourteen now. Promise me that you will take care of your mother."

My heart sank. For months, I had heard about the Great Wall being built to defend the northern border against the Mongols. Tales of the enemy pillaging supply caravans, causing the workers to starve to death, had been swirling through the village.

"The chances of my surviving the harsh working conditions—" My father swallowed the rest of his sentence when my mother came toward us.

A famous saying crept into Ming's mind: "The Great Wall was built on workers' bones."

Metallic crackling interrupted his thoughts. A man's voice spilled out from the loudspeakers scattered around the village. "Good morning, comrades! Time to work. Let your actions show your support for our glorious Revolution and make our benevolent leader, Chairman Mao, proud."

Ming sighed heavily and stood up. "Sorry. I have to go."

Shí's eyes darted around. "What's happening? Who's talking?"

"That's the Political Officer—he's the leader of our village. I'll explain later." Ming stuffed his books into his schoolbag and hurried toward the door.

"Really? Abandoning me already?" Shí sounded indignant.

Ming hesitated, turned, and looked at Shí, wringing his hands anxiously. "I can't be late for school. Last time, my teacher complained to my bā ba, and he was upset with me for days."

"All right. I will wait. It's not like I can wander off anyway." Shí arched an eyebrow at his broken parts.

Ming thought for a moment, then ran back to the desk and picked up the head. Carefully, he placed it in front of the radio.

"Here, this should keep you entertained. You might even learn something."

Switching on the heavy dial, Ming waited for the radio to flicker to life. Suddenly, a revolutionary song poured out of the cracked speaker.

The east is red, the sun rises.

From China arises Mao Zedong.

He strives for the people's happiness . . .

The head stared at the radio, mouth agape.

Ming grabbed his heavy cotton jacket and hurried out of the house.

The weak sun was feebly attempting to banish the dark clouds in the sky. A stiff wind brought the stale smell of burning coal and cooked rice. Tiny snowflakes sifted through the air. Ming locked the courtyard gate behind him and ran toward the west side of the village.

By the time he could see the red flags waving from the roof of the concrete schoolhouse, Ming was out of breath. He stumbled past the pride of Red Star, the tallest sculpture of Chairman Mao within nine miles, in the courtyard.

Inside the schoolhouse, children were singing at the top of their lungs.

March on, march forward, revolutionary youth!
March on, march forward, revolutionary successors!
Victory is calling,
The red flag is guiding . . .

Ming experienced a familiar sinking feeling in his stomach.

Along the great revolutionary path opened by our forefathers,

Push forth the wheel of history.

The morning's political singing had already started and he was late, again.

Mankind grows stronger in stormy wind and waves,

And revolution progresses in raging flames.

It was now or never. Ming stopped in front of a door with a wooden sign inscribed GRADE 7. He cracked the door open, hoping to slip unnoticed into his seat in a corner.

A typical village classroom during the Mao period.

Facing the future,

Taking responsi–

A middle-aged woman in a baggy green Mao-style uniform standing in front of the class made a chopping motion with her arm, abruptly cutting off the singing.

"Ah! Look who has decided to join us!" she sneered.

The large bags under her eyes always reminded Ming of the pandas at the Xi'an zoo.

"Sorry, Teacher Pand—Zhu. I was . . . um . . . helping my father."

"I don't want to hear your excuses!" Teacher Panda waved her hand dismissively.

A few girls giggled softly. Ming slouched to his seat.

"Look at the holes in his shoes," a girl with red cheeks said to the boy sitting behind her, loud enough for the entire class to hear. "Where did they come from? It's not like he ever works in the fields!"

"Good observation, Hua!" Teacher Panda mocked. "He must have worn them out walking to the teahouse."

Everyone broke into laughter.

Head down, Ming dropped his bag onto the desk in front of him and pulled out his English textbook.

Teacher Panda waited for the commotion to die down before addressing the class. "That's enough singing for today. Let's review how to greet comrades in English. Hua, why don't you lead today's practice?"

The red-cheeked girl jumped up and skipped to the front of the class. Ming wondered why Teacher Panda always rewarded the students who were mean to him. Was it because he wasn't from a working-class family?

"Hello, Revolutionary Comrade. How do you do?" The red-cheeked girl's voice rose an octave, making her sound like a leaky balloon.

"Fine. How do you do, Revolutionary Comrade?" the class chorused back.

Ming rifled through his bag. He'd accidentally brought along his bā ba's notebook, which had the same black plastic cover as his. They had been gifts from Comrade Gu, the director of the Xi'an museum.

Hiding the notebook under his desk, Ming flipped through it and found some folded yellow pages.

Red Cheeks: *"Revolutionary Comrade, how are you?"*

Students: *"Very well. How are you, Revolutionary Comrade?"*

As Ming unfolded the pages, he noticed tiny holes along the crease lines. The pages appeared to have come from an old textbook. They were heavily worn, with dark smudges that obscured some of the words. The text on the upper half of one page was lost in brown stains. The ink on the lower half was smeared, but the words remained legible.

. . . who has studied his reign believes that Emperor Qin initially planned to have his ministers and army accompany him to the afterlife. However, his chief consul, Li Si, convinced him that clay soldiers would last much longer than their human counterparts and were thus superior alternatives.

Red Cheeks: *"Wash face, Young Comrade!"*
Students: *"Have you face wash, Young Comrade?"*

In the margin someone had scribbled, "Li Si was a hypocrite. He didn't want to leave his comfortable lifestyle." Ming chuckled.

For thirty-six years, Li Si oversaw the construction of eight thousand clay soldiers.

Eight thousand? There were only three hundred people in Red Star, but whenever Ming went to the village store, he always had to wait in a long line. He grinned, imagining eight thousand terra-cotta soldiers tearing apart the shelves, scattering ginger candy left and right as they fought over the eggs and meat.

Red Cheeks: *"Homework!"*

Students: *"Have you homework finished, Young Comrade?"*

Brave Qin soldiers were chosen as models. Sculptors were sent to the battlefront to take molds of soldiers' faces.

Red Cheeks: *"Stir-fry!"*

Students: *"Have you eat stir-fry yet, Revolutionary Comrade?"*

To speed up the process, the sculptors created eight basic designs. They used them to mass-produce arms, legs, and torsos. Initially, the parts were solid. However, the top-heavy statues couldn't be balanced upright, and so they were hollowed out.

Looking around, Ming pictured all of his classmates having the same bodies and different heads. The girls would look even less attractive with bony arms and flat chests.

The early batches of terra-cotta soldiers were baked whole. But when the temperature reached 1,000°C, they exploded. After many experiments, the sculptors learned to bake the soldiers in pieces before assembling them.

Stacks of unassembled terra-cotta soldiers.

Red Cheeks: *"Mumble mumble mumble."*

Students: *"Mumble."*

"Do you think so, Ming?" A piece of chalk pelted Ming's forehead, snapping him back to reality.

Ming had no idea what the question was. He chuckled nervously. "Uh . . . I hope so."

The red-cheeked girl threw back her head in laughter.

"Lazy city parasite!" Teacher Panda shouted shrilly.

Stir-fry. Wasn't that the last phrase he had heard? Why should he care? He had no food to stir-fry.

Ming looked at the boy sitting next to him, who was about to whisper something when Teacher Panda called out, "Don't talk to him! Ming, go stand in the back!"

Ming's face burned with shame. He stuffed his notebook into his bag, hunched over, and shuffled to the back.

Leaning against the cold wall, Ming thought that he might have a few friends if Teacher Panda didn't always yell at anyone who spoke to him. Would she dislike him less if he hadn't challenged her?

Two years ago, the villagers had followed Mao's command: "Dig tunnels deep, store grain, and prepare for war." They had dug tunnels in the fields, in the village square, in the school's playground, and even inside their homes, crafting hiding places and storing food in preparation for the inevitable Soviet attack.

One day in class, Ming had asked Teacher Panda, "Why would the Soviets want to bomb this tiny village?"

"Why do you want to eat three meals a day?" she had asked icily. "Are you questioning our Great Leader's judgment?"

Since then, she often used Ming as an example of someone who was arrogant and lazy.

Despite Teacher Panda's steadfast belief in Chairman Mao, the Soviet attack never came. What did come were intriguing artifacts—ancient bronze swords and arrowheads—that popped out of the newly dug tunnels like bamboo shoots after a spring rain, prompting the government to establish an outpost for the Xi'an museum in Red Star to streamline the processing of relics between the village and the city. After three months of working in the fields, Ming's bā ba had convinced the museum to grant him the outpost's archaeologist position.

It was a long morning for Ming. He had to stand through all his classes: English, Communist Revolutionary History, Political Studies, and Math. He wished they taught something interesting at school, like ancient history or electronic circuitry. He was so relieved when the Political Officer's voice boomed over the loudspeaker, "Good afternoon, Revolutionary Comrades! Lunchtime!"

He snatched up his schoolbag and made for the door.

"Ming, turn in your homework!" Teacher Panda yelled after him.

Ming ignored her and raced out, brushing past his classmates.

5
THE TEAHOUSE

THE DELICATE SNOWFLAKES HAD TURNED TO HEAVY cotton balls. They clung to Ming's face, becoming droplets of water. The wind had picked up, and it cut through his jacket, chilling him to the bone.

Ming's mind whirled like a rewinding cassette tape. He remembered a conversation his parents had had on a cold, snowy day like this, shortly before his mother's death.

"If only you had shown more enthusiasm for the Revolution, we might still be in the city!" his mother had said, her knitting needles clicking rapidly.

Bā ba's bitter voice had dropped a pitch. "Oh, really? Then why did they send my colleagues away too? Mao just hates all intellectuals!"

Mother had hushed him, glancing out the window nervously. "Don't say that! You know what happens to people who talk like that. They disappear!"

Ming blew on his numb fingers and rubbed them together to restore circulation. He hurried along the only paved road in the village, heading toward home. Bracketed by Li Mountain to the north and the Wei River to the south, Red Star curved from west to east before tapering off in the foothills.

Snow was starting to encrust the roofs of the gray mud houses that lined the road. The houses were spaced evenly apart, and most had an enclosed front yard. Ming stopped outside one without a fence. Despite the heavy cotton flaps hanging over the door, he could smell the mouthwatering scent of roasted peanuts. The characters Chá Guǎn, 茶馆, teahouse, were painted on a wooden board that hung above the doorway.

Bā ba and Ming often visited the only teahouse in Red Star. Ming enjoyed listening to the elders' stories, which grew more outlandish as the hours passed and the piles of empty plates grew taller. His favorite tales were about tomb robbers, secret traps, and fierce battles. The mystical accounts of the first Emperor and his mausoleum had fueled his passion for history.

Pausing now to inhale the aroma, Ming wished he had one yuán, 元, to buy a bag of roasted peanuts or even soybeans. He peered through the window and saw groups of elderly men huddled around four tables covered with chipped teacups and peanut shells. Next to a small wooden stage, a large tin teakettle sat atop a stove that was three times bigger than the one at Ming's home. A spindly old man, eyes half closed, was playing a song from the revolutionary opera *White-Haired Girl* on an èr hú, a two-stringed bow instrument. The man standing next

A typical rural village teahouse of the 1970s.

to him, who was as thin as a chopstick, was circling his hands in the air in time with the music and singing along.

The debts that crushed the working class will be erased . . .

Someone gripped Ming's shoulder. Startled, Ming spun around. It was the village carpenter. The wrinkles on the man's grinning face reminded Ming of a dry, cracked riverbed.

"Come inside and tell us about what the Gee brothers brought you!"

Ming allowed himself to be led in. The aromas of warm tea and roasted peanuts washed over him. His hunger intensified.

All the old men in the teahouse looked up at the newcomers.

One thousand years of feudalism are now uprooted and ended . . .

The singer stopped, his arms held before him as if he were cradling a large watermelon.

The èr hú player opened his eyes. He saw Ming and called out excitedly, "Ming! I heard the Gee brothers found a broken clay soldier from Emperor Qin's tomb. Is it true?"

Ming shrugged. "I don't know."

One of the men sitting nearby broke into laughter, spraying tiny bits of peanut over his table. "Why would Emperor Qin bury a broken clay soldier in his mausoleum?"

"To guard his treasure, you old fool!" the singer called out.

"And why would he need that? Haven't you heard the stories about his mechanical crossbows and his secret traps?" asked the village carpenter as he took an empty seat. "His deadly traps would surely kill any intruders."

Ming briefly felt the urge to tell them about the talking head. Could Shí *really* have come from the Qin tomb? For a long time he had been skeptical that such an incredible monument could be so close to this small village and had often fantasized about the various ways tomb robbers would be killed by the traps. He wondered: If he and Bā ba ever found the tomb, would Bā ba know how to disable them?

The èr hú player pointed his finger at the crowd. "I

have told you people the story many times! There is a vast underground palace, and it's near here!"

The carpenter waved his hands in mock fright. "And a vast terra-cotta army that will kill anyone who breaks in, right?"

The singer stepped off the stage and floated his hand through the air. "Just imagine sailing on Emperor Qin's eternally flowing rivers of mercury!"

"Āī yo! The mercury would kill you long before you got close to it!" The èr hú player clucked his tongue. "I would much rather take a stroll through his orchard of jeweled trees."

"And maybe grab a few jade pears or peaches for your own grave along the way?" teased the carpenter, cracking open a peanut with his teeth.

A few of the men chuckled.

The èr hú player beckoned to Ming. "Come! Let me buy you a bag of peanuts for troubling you to fix my radio again! I couldn't sleep at night without it on."

Ming's stomach grumbled, but he wanted to be polite. He held up his hands. "Oh, it was no trouble at all! I should get home."

The singer piped up, "You're too skinny, Ming! You

should eat more." He walked over and offered Ming a small paper bag.

Ming smiled weakly. "I'm fine, really. Thank you!" Before he could back away, the singer stuffed the bag into Ming's pocket.

"Hey, Ming, my alarm clock stopped working," a man with a long white beard called out from across the room. "Could you take a look at it? I brought it with me in case you came by today."

"Sure! I'll give it a try," Ming said warmly.

The men in the room eagerly helped pass the clock to Ming. Behind the dusty glass, a red hen and three yellow chicks fashioned from metal were frozen mid-peck. Ming stuffed it into his bag and walked toward the door.

"Wait! The back of my watch is loose again." A toothless man took a watch from his pocket and held it out to Ming.

"I can tighten it for you now." Ming took the watch and fished out a small screwdriver from his pocket. A few moments later, he handed the watch back to the man. "That should fix it!"

"Thank you, clever boy! Say hello to your father for me."

"You're welcome! I will."

Ming liked these old men. Unlike the Gee brothers and Teacher Panda, they were always nice to him. When he fixed their broken watches, radios, and flashlights, it made him feel useful and happy, especially when Bā ba told him how proud he was of him.

Ming hefted his schoolbag. "Bye now!"

As he backed out into the cold, all the old men waved to him.

6

JOINING THE QIN ARMY

BY THE TIME MING GOT HOME, HE WAS COLD AND hungry. He leaned his shoulder against the front gate and dug out his key. He heard a strange noise coming from inside. He opened the gate and stepped into the courtyard. Before he ran into the house, he quickly slammed the door shut and barred it.

Shí was still on the desk, rocking in time to the music coming from the radio. Ming hastily shut the door. He winced as Shí growled out "The East Is Red" in a gravelly, off-key voice.

A typical village of the 1970s.

Chairman Mao loves the people.

He guides us to build a new China.

Ming knew that the radio station repeated the same "revolutionary" songs when it wasn't broadcasting political speeches. He had no doubt that Shí had spent the day listening to—and memorizing—popular songs like "Socialism Is Good" and "No Communist Party, No New China."

Shí looked up. "Ah, you're back! How was school?"

"Fine." Ming reached over and snapped off the radio. He dropped his schoolbag and pulled a battered box of matches from his pocket. With a flick, he lit a piece of old newspaper and threw it onto the coals in the stove.

Shí followed Ming's movements closely. "Hmm . . . A tiny twig can start a fire. Another modern miracle!"

"Yeah, they're great." Too hungry to explain how the matches worked, Ming slipped them back into his pocket and put on the teakettle.

"In my day, we had to use iron and rocks." Shí tilted his chin at the radio. "And this magic box is just incredible! How did your people squeeze in so many musicians?"

"Like you said—it's magic." Ming walked into the back room and placed the old man's broken clock on the table next to his bed. Even though he had eaten the peanuts on the walk home, his stomach still rumbled wildly.

Ming decided to distract himself, as he often did when he was hungry. He returned to the front room and slumped down in the chair beside the desk. "So tell me, Shí, why would the Emperor need a Great Wall? Didn't he have a large army?"

"He did, but it wasn't big enough to guard the entire border. Haven't your books taught you about the Mongols?

They attacked and then vanished like smoke in the wind, leaving behind burning villages and bloody corpses."

Ming changed the subject, as he had very little knowledge about the Mongols. "Was it hard being at home without your father?"

"Yes. The worst part was listening to my mother sobbing at night. I felt so powerless."

"I know the feeling." Ming nodded sympathetically. He had rarely seen Bā ba smile since his mother's death. "Did you get drafted into the Qin Army?"

"No, I was too young."

"Then how did you get in?"

"I volunteered—to save my father. Thanks to my mother's good cooking, I'd grown tall and sturdy." Shí smacked his lips, as if once again savoring his mother's delicious food. "The recruiter was looking for strong men and believed I was fifteen." Shí grinned. "He was a year off."

Ming wished that he were from a working-class family and could volunteer for the People's Liberation Army. He heard the soldiers ate meat and fish every day!

"What happened to your mother? Didn't your father ask you to take care of her?"

"There was nothing I could do." Ming detected a note

of sadness in Shí's voice. "I tried everything, but I couldn't feed us. I volunteered because I heard that the Emperor would reward brave soldiers with land and excuse their family members from construction duty. I thought capturing a few Mongol heads would be easy. I should have known better."

"Mongol heads?" Confused, Ming asked, "What do you mean?"

"Qin soldiers received rewards based on the number of enemies we killed. At the end of the battle, we turned in the heads to be tallied."

Ming's attention was abruptly caught by deep voices outside. He couldn't make out what they were saying. He got up and looked out the window. The heavy wooden gate was still securely barred.

"It broke my heart to leave my thin, frail mother behind," Shí continued. "The night before my departure, she was hunched over a flickering oil lamp, sewing. Through half-closed eyes, I watched tears roll down her wrinkled face. Her lips moved silently as her fingers worked the needle. Legend says that if a soldier wears a jacket made with one thousand stitches, he will be protected from harm. I was not sure if she was counting or praying to the kitchen god."

Ming's eyes welled up with tears and he sat back down.

Shí paused and looked at him with concern.

"My mother knitted the warmest sweaters for me when she was alive," Ming said in a choked voice. The rest of the words stuck in his throat like a fish bone.

"You must miss her," Shí said softly.

Ming nodded. He was too embarrassed to tell Shí that he often woke up at night and clutched the blue sweater that his mother had left behind, breathing in her familiar smell. But the scent had grown faint, so faint that he worried he was only imagining it. The memories of his mother had been slipping from his mind like rain running off a glazed tile. Sometimes he found forgetfulness easier than dwelling on the past.

Someone pounded on the courtyard gate. Ming sighed. It was probably the Gee brothers again. He hoped that if he ignored them long enough, they would go away.

The next morning I left my mother. I was wearing my new jacket. It had a round shield stitched on the front and a pine tree, the symbol for a long life, on the back. To my surprise, many of the new recruits were around my age.

After three days of hard marching, we arrived at our

camp in the eastern part of Liaoning Province. I was standing in line collecting my supplies when someone punched my shoulder.

"Shí!"

It was Feng, a boy from my village with whom I had often raced horses.

"How long have you been here?" I asked excitedly.

"Two days! It's great to see you!"

Feng told me that with so many men like my father off building the Great Wall and the Emperor's mausoleum, the recruiters had loosened the age restrictions.

The leather armor I received had a large patch of dried blood staining the chest. It resembled a blossoming peony, with a hole the size of an arrowhead at the heart.

"I hope you have better luck than the previous owner," Feng joked.

"I am protected!" I proudly patted the jacket my mother had sewn.

The banging had stopped, but Ming could hear voices arguing heatedly out on the street.

That night, rain and wind whipped at our tent. Cold

and hungry, I huddled under my thin cotton blanket. My dreams were haunted by images of the gruesome death of my armor's previous owner.

"Get up! Gather outside!"

The harsh yelling woke me. As we stumbled out into the dark, icy rain lashed at our faces. Chilled to the bone and shivering with fear, I watched a platoon of veterans march in.

"Look at their beat-up armor!" Feng said under his breath. "They must have just come from a fierce battle."

Even though the men looked exhausted, they stood tall. From the pride in their eyes and the sneers on their lips, it was apparent that they looked down on us new recruits.

The camp commander barked at our disheveled lines, "Pair off with a veteran and follow his orders!"

I was about to tell Feng that we should stay together, when a large man stopped in front of me. A scar ran from his temple down to the base of his neck. I noticed that several of his teeth were missing.

"I am Liang. Come with me!" He turned abruptly and stomped off.

I hurried after him.

"Stay alive!" Feng called out.

"You too!" I shouted back.

Liang wasn't a friendly or talkative person. He was one of those rare men who could terrify you with a look. My only consolation was that he seemed to dislike everyone equally. For a week, our squad of three veterans and three recruits marched across rugged mountain terrain to get to our first posting, which was located on a newly completed section of the Great Wall in the far north.

Life was harsh and food was scarce. Our main staple was sorghum. We ate sorghum porridge, sorghum cake, and sorghum noodles. When Liang and I managed to get our hands on some meat and eggs, we would cook together.

Ming's mouth watered.

One day we marched for hours, with only a small bowl of sorghum porridge for lunch. At our campsite that evening, Liang and I built a fire, huddling close for its warmth.

"Set your helmet over the fire," he ordered.

I hesitated, unsure of what was happening.

"Now!" He was irritated by my reluctance.

I hastily used two thick sticks to prop my helmet over the fire. To my surprise, he turned the helmet upside down and tossed in a handful of onions and some chunks of dried meat. Then he emptied the water from his cow-stomach canteen into the helmet.

The delicious steam soon set my head swirling and my stomach dancing.

Ming gulped. It had been so long since he had smelled meat cooking.

"Uh . . . I thought helmets were supposed to be worn in battle," I commented nervously.

Liang snorted. "Only cowards wear helmets and armor. Brave Qin soldiers shed unnecessary weight so they can charge quickly and hit the enemy hard."

"Are you going to teach me how to fight?" I asked tentatively.

Liang stared at me for a long moment and said, "That would be a waste of my time."

I was afraid to ask what he meant. Did he think I'd die quickly?

After that, any offhand remark from him or a sick joke by another soldier became a bad omen. I kept picturing my impending death.

"Ming! Give us back our earth god!" The harsh tones, accompanied by heavy pounding, cut through the cold air.

Ming jumped up. "Be quiet! Someone is outside." As he headed into the courtyard, he tried to think of some excuse to send the visitors away.

Ming swung open the gate and found two of the Gee brothers standing there. The oldest Gee brother's fist was raised, poised to pound on the gate again. When he saw Ming, the man lowered his hand and smiled sheepishly.

"What do you want?" Ming tried to sound stern. He was irritated that he had to deal with the Gee brothers again.

"Why did you bar your gate in the middle of the day?" barked the youngest brother.

"Why are you trying to break into my courtyard?" Ming shot back. It was people like the Gee brothers who made him hate the village.

"Give us back the earth god!" demanded the old man.

The youngest brother tried to squeeze by. Ming blocked the entry with his thin frame, taking up a defiant posture: one foot forward, one foot behind, so that his upper body slouched backward.

"What does this look like to you—the communal toolshed?" Ming raised his voice and fixed a hard gaze on the brothers. "The 'earth god' is the property of the state. You'll have to manage without it." He was pleased with his quick response.

"But—but—but I need it for my daughter-in-law!" the oldest brother protested. "She's about to have a baby, and I want the earth god to protect her!"

With gritted teeth, Ming listened to the oldest Gee brother babble. He watched the loose skin of the man's chin wobble as he spoke.

"Wait here," Ming said at last.

He went back into the house and rooted around in one of the desk drawers. When he found what he was looking for, he turned around, only to find that the brothers had followed him in and were staring at the now-inanimate head.

Ming stepped in front of the head, blocking it from the farmers' view. "Look at this. See the red seal?" He held the piece of paper in front of their faces, pointing at a line halfway down the paper. "It's from the government. Right here, it says, 'Any artifacts unearthed are the property of the people and therefore belong to the Xi'an museum.'" Gesturing to the head on the desk, he continued, "This doesn't belong to me or you or my father. It belongs to the people. That means it's illegal for you to take it."

The old man's tone became pleading. "But I *am* one of the people! I just want to borrow the head until my grandson is born!"

Ming lowered the document. Did the old man really believe that Shí was an earth god? Perhaps there was another way of dealing with him. He leaned closer, speaking as he would to a small child. "Listen, I wasn't going to tell you this, but I have been reading about this head since I got home from school." He pointed at a stack of old books on the desk. "Believe me, this isn't the kind of earth god you want watching over your grandson's birth. It's a malicious god."

"You mean . . . a demon?" the oldest brother asked nervously.

"Tsk. 'Demon' is such an ugly word. Let's just call it . . . a 'restless spirit,'" Ming drawled, a smirk playing at the corners of his mouth.

The old man took a quick step back.

Ming whispered conspiratorially, "There's no cause for worry. It looks like it's meditating right now. Let's be careful not to wake it up." With that, he guided the Gee brothers toward the door. "As soon as my father comes home, he'll take it to the city, so it won't bring any bad luck to our peaceful village."

"Oh . . . ah . . . well . . . Yes, in that case, you hold on to it," the oldest brother mumbled. "Besides, even if it was a benevolent earth god, I would never take the people's property." Wearing an uneasy grin, he hustled out.

The youngest brother followed.

Ming closed the gate behind them and heaved a huge sigh of relief.

As he walked back into the house, he heard a rhythmic grinding noise, like a saw cutting gravel. It took him a while to realize that the head was laughing!

"You continue to impress me, Ming! Me, an evil earth god!" The head laughed again.

"Well, do you *want* to watch the village seamstress give birth?" Ming asked.

7
ASSEMBLING

"I BET NO ONE WOULD MISTAKE ME FOR AN EARTH god if I were in one piece," Shí said thoughtfully.

Ming laughed. "Yeah, and if I grew wings, I could fly to Xi'an to find my bā ba."

Shí arched an eyebrow. "What do you mean?"

"I mean, it's easier said than done."

"Is there anywhere you can put me together?"

Ming looked around the crowded room and thought for a moment. "On my bā ba's bed, I guess."

"Then please take all of my parts to the bed and put them in their proper places!"

Ming didn't know what Shí was planning, but so far he'd been full of surprises. He carried the head into the bedroom, which was half the size of the front room. Empty pickle jars, chipped bowls, broken mugs, and mismatched chopsticks covered a rough-hewn table that had never seen a coat of varnish. It stood between the two beds, which were set against opposite walls. A map of Li County covered the entire wall over the bigger bed. Above the smaller bed, Ming had hung a poster of a tiger. Its yellow eyes glowed with cold light, and its scarlet tongue was wet with blood. A young, muscular man with broad shoulders straddled the tiger. His fist was in the air, and his eyes sparkled. Beneath the tiger, a slogan read, "All Counter-Revolutionaries Are Paper Tigers!" In smaller characters it said, "All capitalist countries, like America, are paper tigers—threats without substance."

Ming set the head on the bigger bed and went back to the front room. He loaded the broken body parts into a bamboo basket and dragged it to the bedroom. The head watched him quizzically, but Ming was too hungry to talk, so he avoided eye contact. It took him three trips to gather all the pieces. After unloading them beside the bed, Ming fetched a small brown ceramic jar from the table.

"What's that?" asked Shí curiously.

"Homemade rice glue," Ming said, holding up the jar. "Father uses it to repair broken pots and vases. I'm not sure it will work on you, but it's all I have." He removed the lid and looked inside. "Not much left. If I had some rice, I could make more."

An archaeologist assembling a broken terra-cotta soldier.

The head barked out laughter. "Even if your rice glue worked, you would need a whole bucket just for my legs!

And how do you imagine I am going to move if I'm glued together?"

Ming glared at the head defensively. "Well, then, what do you want me to use? My spit?"

"Arrange me on the bed," instructed Shí. "Make sure I'm aligned correctly."

Ming struggled to drag the heavy limbs onto the bed, scraping them across the wooden frame. He positioned them as best as he could.

Ming set the head flush against the neck. He took a step back to survey his work.

Suddenly, a bright light blinded him, and the house began to shake. One of the wooden bowls rattled and bounced so much that it fell off the table and hit the floor with a hollow clatter.

Ming stood frozen, shielding his eyes.

"You idiot!" Shí's voice was shrill with pain. "You mixed up my legs! Quick, quick! Switch them—now!"

Squinting against the light, Ming could see that Shí was trembling violently. Holding his breath, he forced himself to move to the foot of the shaking bed. He reached over, grabbed hold of Shí's legs, and dragged them away from his torso.

Suddenly, the light dimmed and the thrashing lessened. Ming rolled the leg closer to him over the other. With a pop, they jammed back into position on Shí's torso.

Ming stepped back, ready to run in case the clay soldier exploded or thrashed around again, but the quivering stopped and the light faded. To Ming's surprise, Shí sat up, looked around, and stretched luxuriously. "Much better!"

Shí swung around and carefully put his feet down on the ground. Slowly, he stood up.

Mouth agape, Ming tracked the soldier's movements. Upright, Shí was a full head taller than Ming. A plated armor vest covered his upper torso, leaving his arms and legs covered only by what appeared to be a gown.

Shí swung his arms about. Bits of fine brown dust floated down around him, leaving a thin layer on the floor. "Ah!" he sighed with satisfaction. "Everything seems to be working well. Old Tian did a good job! You see this mark on my neck?" He pointed to the 田 character. "It is my sculptor's signature. As long as it is intact, I can be reassembled like new, even if I am in pieces."

"Er . . . Why did you need my help, then?"

Shí flexed his fingers experimentally. "Because I cannot move my detached parts."

An unearthed terra-cotta soldier.

Ming moved back a few steps and gazed admiringly at the large terra-cotta soldier. "You look . . . very impressive!"

"Thank you! Believe it or not, I used to be even more handsome."

Ming raised an eyebrow skeptically.

"Tian decorated me with lacquer paints made from colorful minerals and egg whites."

"Egg whites?" Ming's stomach gurgled.

"It thickened the paint and protected me from moisture, so my color would last for eternity."

"Well, apparently it didn't work. Or did he run out of every color but gray?"

"I have been around a long time," Shí blustered. "Much has happened!"

8

GUARDING THE GREAT WALL

"SHOULD I CONTINUE MY STORY?" ASKED SHÍ.

Still astounded by the animated statue standing before him, Ming could only nod. He sat down on the edge of his bed and waited eagerly for Shí to resume.

Our guard post on the Great Wall was located on the steep hilltops of the Pamir Mountains, strategically situated to protect the Silk Road, the vital trade route between China and the countries to the west. We were divided into three shifts, taking turns standing guard at the top of the tower and sleeping in our quarters below. From the upper level we could see the distant desert stretching off to dark mountain ranges. Rain was rare, and a steady wind whipped up the sand, often obscuring the surrounding peaks and cliffs in thick, eerie dust storms.

The initial shock had subsided a bit. Ming shifted to make himself comfortable. He reached over to the table for the old man's clock and began fiddling with it.

Rocks the size of my head were piled every few feet along the wall. Next to them were cauldrons filled with oil. At the top of the tower was a big pot of oil, surrounded by damp straw. The first few weeks I stood guard, I kept imagining the pounding of horses' hooves, the shadows of men scaling the wall, and snarling barbarians grabbing my arm to pull me over. Yet the only sound was the desert wind and the occasional exchange between Liang and me, as if we were the only humans for hundreds of miles.

Ming popped the back off the clock and adjusted the tiny gears with his screwdriver. He held the clock to his ear, listening.

"What should I do if the Mongols attack us?" I asked Liang.

He patted my stiff back and said, "They are more likely to attack towers on the lower ground first. As soon as you spot the enemy, light the warning fire. Our brothers below depend on us."

The fact that Liang said little only made me hang on to his words when he did speak. And he was right—for months, I never saw a Mongol up close. Occasionally, when the dust storms subsided, I saw fighting off in the distance.

With a sharp, metallic crackling, the Political Officer's voice suddenly sputtered from the loudspeakers. "Comrades! Set aside your revolutionary work! Come to the teahouse for a special meeting!"

A special meeting? Ming's heart tightened. The last time there had been a special meeting, the village potter had been publicly denounced and sent away. He had not returned. Ming looked at Shí standing tall and straight, wrapped up in his memories.

While other off-duty soldiers stayed below, singing and trading stories, Liang and I spent many nights bent over his homemade game of Go by the light of an oil lamp. Nothing distracted us from our game but the whispering wind and the pattering of sand against the stone walls. I began to appreciate him. I think the feeling was mutual.

Early one morning, Liang let me stand guard alone. As I marveled at the orange sunrise staining the desert sky, my breath caught in my throat. A small dust cloud was racing like a wild dragon toward our tower, growing larger by the second. A mix of excitement and fear shot through my belly.

Ming's bā ba always went to the meetings by himself. With him absent, Ming wondered if he should go alone.

"Attack! Attack!" I yelled. "The enemy's attacking!" I lit the oil in the pot, throwing the damp straw on it to create a thick plume of dark smoke. Within minutes, the signal smoke was swirling into the air like a phoenix's tail over the Great Wall.

My fellow soldiers, roused from their sleep, joined me at the tower. The Mongols were now about half a mile from the wall. Suddenly, our cavalry appeared on the eastern horizon, backlit by the crimson sky. Like a small herd of deer

A contemporary reenactment of lighting signal fires on the watch towers on the Great Wall.

racing from a sea of fire, they caught up with the enemy and smashed through them with lightning speed, hacking left and right. The Mongols were blindsided. Dragging their dead and wounded with them, they scattered like terrified mice. That was the first time I saw Liang smile.

Though he would never admit it, Ming secretly wished he had such an opportunity to impress Teacher Panda. Maybe nothing he did would ever change how she treated him.

"Did Liang praise you for lighting the warning fire?" asked Ming.

"I don't think he was capable of praise, but I could tell he was pleased. He said that often the signal fires were lit too late and the enemy would be long gone by the time our cavalry arrived.

"After the battle, when the cavalry fought like animals for the dead Mongols' heads, Liang's face darkened. 'Lucky dogs!' he growled. 'They're going to get even more land and bigger houses!'"

"I wish we could own a house," Ming said dreamily. "These days, all the property belongs to the socialist communes." Turning to Shí, he asked, "Did they trade the heads at the local market?" He pictured bloody Mongol heads hanging by their hair next to the pig and cow heads at the butcher's stall.

Shí chuckled. "No. At the end of the battle, officers recorded the heads and rewarded each soldier accordingly."

Satisfied, Ming snapped on the back of the clock and placed it on the table. He proudly watched the hen and the three yellow chicks peck at invisible grain as the second hand slowly crept around.

"What's that?"

"A clock. It tells time."

"Oh, it's alive! It hides in a shell like a turtle, but I can hear its heart beating."

"No." Ming chuckled. "It's a machine."

There was a commotion outside the house. *Thump, thump* . . . The knocking sound continued, steady as a drumbeat.

"Meeting at the teahouse!" someone shouted.

Ming stood up, held his breath, and waited until the shuffling footsteps faded into the distance.

Shí looked at him with concern. "What's happening?"

"It's nothing." Ming sat back down. "They're probably

lecturing everyone again on how to act like a true revolutionary. Please go on."

Shí paused for a moment and then continued. "Liang told me that the cavalrymen often bragged about their new land and lavish homes, and of how their family members were excused from mandatory labor. I grew restless, feeling as though I was wasting my time and talent, sitting on the wall and playing countless games of Go."

"Talent?"

"Are you so surprised?" Shí sounded offended. "Back in our village, Feng's father was the best horse trainer. He taught Feng and me to ride at a young age. Even though Feng was better with the girls, I could beat him in a horse race any day."

Ming had never ridden a horse. He wondered if it was harder than riding a bike.

One night, soon after I had lit the warning fire, Liang interrupted my dreams of slaughtering Mongols on a charging brown horse.

"Wake up! Get to the tower!" He shook me violently. "The Mongols are here!"

Half awake, I grabbed my sword and ran out of our

sleeping quarters along with the other soldiers. The warning bonfire and torches illuminated the sky. The night air reeked of smoke and burning oil. It was the attack I had long dreaded, yet eagerly anticipated.

Mongol arrows flew through the smoke. I snuck a quick peek. Enemy soldiers were climbing up the wall on rough pine ladders. Liang suddenly grabbed me and pulled me down. An arrow zipped by, a feather's width from my hair.

"Spread out along the wall! Get the oil ready!" he yelled.

As I ran along the wall, a hand gripped its edge and an enemy head popped up. I matched gazes with a boy about my age. His face was ghostly with a dusting of sand. His dark eyes reflected the flickering light of the torch behind me. I hesitated for a moment before pushing him with all my strength. He screamed as he fell off the wall. Even over the sounds of battle, I thought I heard his head smacking against the rocks far below. At the time, I was too busy fighting, but that boy's terrified face would haunt me for centuries to come.

"Over here!" Liang yelled.

I ran over and helped him upend the cauldron of boiling oil on the Mongols who were scaling the wall like ants climbing a tree. They fell off the ladders, crying out as their

skin melted, and rolled around in agony on the ground. Still another wave rushed up the ladders. Liang and I pushed the ladders off the wall, sending the enemy flying through the air. We rained rocks down atop their heads.

Ming had never imagined that fighting on the Great Wall was so brutal. He looked forward to telling these stories to the old men in the teahouse. He could just picture them spitting tea across the table in disbelief.

"The Mongols were a determined bunch," Shí muttered musingly. "By the time our cavalry arrived, we had run out of oil and rocks and were defending the wall with spears, crossbows, and swords."

"Didn't Liang say that the Mongols would attack only the lower towers?"

Shí looked impressed. "Ha, you paid attention, young man! That's correct. But they changed their tactics when the weather grew cold. The Mongols desperately wanted to capture our supplies, so they attacked indiscriminately. Believe it or not, I secretly wished they would succeed in getting onto the wall. That way I would have a chance to lop off their heads, claim my rewards, and free my father."

"Why didn't you just go down after the battle to collect a few heads?" Ming imagined farmers out in the fields harvesting watermelons.

"We couldn't."

"Why not?"

Ming heard rough voices outside and then heavy pounding on the gate. He stood up.

"We were prohibited from leaving our post," answered Shí. "The cavalrymen knew that too. To mock us, they would wave the heads at us. That was when I vowed to join them."

There was a sharp crash. Startled, Ming jumped up. The front gate had been kicked open! From the voices and the sounds in the courtyard, he could tell that the intruders were angry. He hurried to the door and saw men and women swarming inside the cramped courtyard, muddying the fresh snow.

The older villagers hung back, craning their necks to see over the crowd. Runny-nosed children in old woolen shirts crammed over bulky jackets jostled one another to get in front for a good view. Ming recognized several of his classmates gathered around Teacher Panda. At the head of the crowd were the three Gee brothers, with their wheelbarrow.

Ming stood defiantly on the stoop and tried to sound authoritative. "What do you want? Get out of here!"

But when he spotted a skinny man standing at the back of the crowd, his chest deflated.

9
THE POLITICAL OFFICER

THE MAN WAS THE POLITICAL OFFICER OF RED STAR. He had the features of a goat, with obsidian eyes and a sloping forehead that even his Mao-style hat couldn't hide. An old pistol hung from his hip inside a leather holster. He was silently observing Ming, wearing the familiar, shameless grin that Ming often saw when the man accepted "gifts" from him.

On the fifteenth of every month, when Ming's bā ba received his salary of sixty yuán, Ming would go to the village shop and buy a pound of meat or a dozen eggs, which he would then deliver to the Political Officer's house. Every time he walked out of the shop, Ming imagined the mouthwatering dishes he could have shared with his bā ba if only they had been able to keep the food for themselves.

The snow had stopped, and the sun now peeked out from behind the clouds, shining weakly onto the gathered crowd. The Political Officer pushed a young militiaman wearing a red armband and ordered, "Go! Get this so-called earth god! I want to see it!"

The crowd quickly parted, making way for the militiaman and the Political Officer. The Gee brothers inched forward behind them.

Ming's palms grew sweaty. He tried to imagine himself as a revolutionary hero from a movie, facing down a horde of enemies.

The militiaman, with pimple scars on his cheeks, approached him.

"H-h-hold on," said Ming. "You have to wait until my father comes home." He nervously ran his fingers through his disheveled hair, disgusted by the pleading tone of his own voice.

The Political Officer abruptly spat on the ground,

grinding the spit beneath his shoe. He pushed the militiaman aside and snarled at Ming, "I know how that little abacus clicks away in your head. Playing tough with me won't work!"

He turned to face the crowd, spreading his arms and smiling broadly. "As your Political Officer, it is my responsibility to educate you. Don't believe that old feudal nonsense. There is no god in new China... only our dear Chairman Mao!" Spittle flew from between his yellow teeth.

Ming was now drenched in sweat, as if someone had poured a bowl of cold water down his back collar. He felt his throat tighten. It took effort to draw air into his lungs. He thought back to when Richard Nixon, the President of the United States, had visited Beijing the previous year. Chairman Mao had replaced his command "Dig tunnels" with "Establish diplomatic channels." And so the farmers had stopped digging like squirrels in autumn, and the flood of artifacts had quickly trickled down to a feeble stream of a few old bricks here and there, some broken pots, and the occasional chunk of carved stone.

Then, two months ago, the museum had stopped paying Bā ba, and they had run out of money to buy Goat Face "gifts." Their "lack of generosity" hadn't gone unnoticed, and Goat Face had paid them a visit. "Why is it, Old Chen," he had asked Ming's bā ba, "that you still haven't found anything valuable? I have a theory. I think you're selling artifacts on the black market! That wouldn't be difficult, would it? It's not like honest, working-class farmers could identify anything of value."

After sharing his theory, the Political Officer had picked up the two boiled sweet potatoes meant for their dinner and stalked out.

Ming knew that stealing from the state was punishable by death, and that evidence was rarely required for prosecution.

The following night, after eating a bowl of watery rice congee, Ming's bā ba had left for the Political Officer's house with their last remaining family treasure.

Tucked under his arm was a cardboard box lined with blue silk. In it was an earth-colored ginseng root from which emanated a strong medicinal smell. Ming's uncle, a ginseng picker, had sent it when he heard that his sister, Ming's mother, had fallen ill with bronchitis.

Ming had seen the ginseng. It had round knobs at the top and tendrils branching out from the sides like arms and legs, which made it look like a wrinkled baby. Bā ba

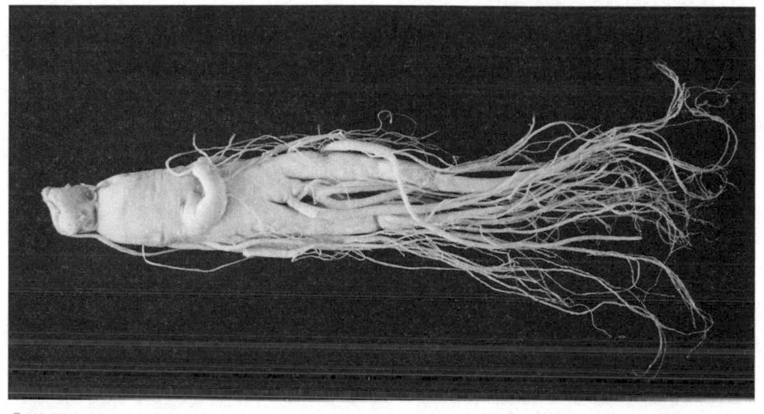

A ginseng root.

had told him that it took decades for a root to grow that thick; ginseng was a superior tonic for strengthening the body, and even Emperors had used it.

They had kept the root in remembrance of Ming's mother and as a safeguard against bad spirits. Now that it was gone, Ming couldn't think of any valuables to bribe Goat Face with. Despite that, he decided that he couldn't just let him take Shí.

Ming took a step forward. With feigned confidence he said, "This office belongs to the Xi'an museum. So the 'earth god' is the property of the museum. You can't take it!"

The crowd murmured. Ming wasn't sure if they agreed or were surprised by his boldness.

Goat Face ignored Ming's speech. He raised a hand

and silenced the villagers. "I know that your father is in Xi'an begging to keep his job!" In a sneering tone he asked, "Who here remembers seeing any *important* discoveries?"

High up in the branches of the hawthorn tree, two sparrows chirped. Their peeping filling the silent courtyard.

"What about you?" Goat Face pointed to the middle Gee brother, who answered by shaking his head. "Me, neither! What if I told you that there actually have been *many* important discoveries and Old Chen's been selling them to his bourgeois cronies on the black market!"

Ming's head swam. What the Political Officer was saying was a blatant lie. He knew that his bā ba had sent everything—even the smallest broken piece of pottery—to the museum.

"I have known this for a long time and was waiting for the right moment to reveal his crime," Goat Face continued, turning and emphasizing his words with a gesture toward Ming. "Old Chen has been hiding treasures from us! How else could he be so confident that the Emperor's tomb is nearby . . . and yet have nothing to show for it after two years?"

Ming felt as if his heart were being stir-fried in a hot pan. His nostrils flared and his eyes were filled with rage.

Murmuring broke out among the villagers. Ming looked up and saw the èr hú player and the singer. They quickly looked away, but he thought he caught a glimmer of sympathy in the old men's eyes.

The Political Officer raised an eyebrow, glanced at the crowd, and continued. "Like the old proverb says: After the water drains from the river, the stones will emerge. Just imagine! After making a fortune from selling our glorious country's treasures on the black market, Old Chen now has the nerve to go demand that the city museum pay him a salary. As soon as he comes back, we'll hold a public denouncement meeting."

Ming felt his knees could no longer support his weight. Last year, the village potter had complained to two visiting city officials about the Political Officer "borrowing" his best pots and never returning them. Little did he know that the Political Officer had actually given the pots to the officials as gifts. A week later, after the Political Officer had held a public denouncement meeting, the potter had been sent on a truck to build terraced rice fields. He had yet to return. Word was that he'd died.

"Go get the earth god!" ordered the Political Officer.

The Gee brothers brushed past Ming. Goat Face and the militiaman followed close behind. Heart thumping, Ming realized that he had to act quickly, not stand like a dumbstruck chicken. He squeezed between the brothers and blocked the bedroom doorway by gripping the sides and planting his feet like bamboo stakes.

The youngest Gee brother pulled at his arm. Ming didn't budge.

Goat Face brushed the Gee brother aside. "Let me deal with this!" He backhanded Ming across the face.

The force of the blow snapped Ming's head back. He collided with the door frame and fell to the floor. He tasted something warm and salty. As he reached for his face, which felt like someone had pressed a hot iron on it, he heard shouts of disbelief from the back room.

"What's this?" roared the Political Officer. "You said it was just a head and some broken body parts!"

"Wh-wh-what happened? How did all those pieces come together?" cried the middle Gee brother.

"Take it to my house! Now!" ordered Goat Face.

The Gee brothers and the militiaman dragged Shí out

of the bedroom. The terra-cotta soldier was now as stiff as a signpost.

"How did that scrawny runt move this thing?" the youngest brother said with a grimace. "It's heavier than your lazy son!"

The oldest brother growled unintelligibly and bumped into the teakettle, sending it flying. Hot water spilled all over the floor. A slew of papers scattered across the room like feathers shed by an alarmed chicken.

Ming tried to get up, but his vision blurred, and the room spun. He fell to the ground and groaned weakly. Darkness embraced him.

At the sight of the terra-cotta statue, the crowd in the courtyard erupted excitedly, like a pot of boiling porridge.

"Go home! Go home!" shouted the Political Officer. "The special meeting is over. We'll resume when Old Chen gets back."

The crowd made way for the Gee brothers and the militiaman, who loaded Shí in the wheelbarrow. The villagers followed them through the gate, chattering and clicking their tongues in amazement.

The Gee brothers grunted as they dragged and pushed

the wheelbarrow. It wobbled unsteadily through the dirty snow on its flat tire, leaving a trail in its wake. The militiaman ran up to the side to steady Shí's legs.

"Be careful! Don't break it!" the Political Officer yelled.

The group passed a wall painted with Mao's slogans and turned east. A curious crowd, mostly women and children, followed at a safe distance. The Political Officer turned and pointed at them.

"We can't build a modern Communist China by standing around. Go study our Great Leader's teachings!"

The villagers stopped in their tracks right in the middle of the street. With heads bowed and shoulders slumped, they turned and walked away silently.

A village wall painted with a revolutionary slogan, a common sight during Mao's reign. It reads, "Arm our minds with Chairman Mao's teachings."

10
DYNAMITE

A SINGLE WHITE CLOUD SHAPED LIKE A STEAMED bun hung heavily in the pale, translucent sky. Cooking fires cast an orange glow upon the village. The aroma of dinner being prepared filled the air: a mixture of acrid smoke from burning coal, cooked rice, stewing meat, and pungent garlic and ginger stir-fried in pig fat.

Houses near the edge of Red Star were similar to those in the center—single-story mud huts with courtyards—except here there was more space between the properties.

The group of men struggling with the wheelbarrow

stopped at the only two-story house. The setting sun cast a yellow glow on its red ceramic-tiled roof and the high brick walls that separated the house from the quiet road.

The Political Officer's wife—a round-cheeked woman resembling an overfed rabbit—greeted them at the gate and ushered them in. The courtyard, paved with slabs of dark stone, was at least three times bigger than Ming's. Ears of corn and dried red peppers hung from the eaves. Disturbed by the visitors, chickens skittered across the yard, seeking hiding places around a wooden shed fit snugly in one corner.

"Inside, inside!" the Political Officer instructed.

The men half carried, half dragged Shí out of the wheelbarrow and into the house. They propped him up next to the entrance to the big living room. The opposite wall had a large square window that overlooked a field. In front of the window was a brightly varnished wooden table and four high-backed chairs. On the wall to the left, a smiling portrait of Chairman Mao hung above a gas stove, an unusual luxury in the village. Four large armchairs made of rare sandalwood were arranged in a semicircle around the stove. Delicately embroidered cushions softened their hard outlines.

The Gee brothers stared at the pantry next to the window. It was stuffed with vegetables, eggs, sausages, smoked fish, and dried mushrooms.

"Stay away from where you dug up the statue," the Political Officer said harshly, shoving the brothers away from the pantry. "Your new well has to be on the west side of the village." He waved them out of the house as if he were shooing away mosquitoes.

The Political Officer whispered something to the militiaman and walked him out into the courtyard. The man nodded like an obedient student and hurried off.

When Goat Face returned, he saw that the table had been set for dinner. Bowls, chopsticks, and small glasses surrounded a plate of fried peanuts and a large jar of three-flower liquor.

Goat Face's wife brought out a plate of thin-sliced roasted beef garnished with red peppers and chopped peanuts, bathed in soy-ginger sauce. She waited until the Political Officer had chewed a mouthful of the tender beef before speaking.

"Is that what they dug up?" she asked, looking over at Shí. "I heard it was just a head and some broken pieces! Is it worth much?"

"It doesn't matter." The Political Officer pointed at Shí with his chopsticks. A few drops of dark sauce dripped onto the table. "If the old men at the teahouse are right, it came from Emperor Qin's tomb. One way or the other, we'll find out tonight."

"Just be careful!" The woman left the room and returned shortly with a small bowl of deep-fried soybeans. "Will we make enough money to buy a color TV? I've dreamed of the day when I could watch people singing and dancing without leaving my home!"

Goat Face snatched a handful of soybeans, ignoring the two that slipped out of his grip and fell to the floor. "If all goes according to plan, I'll be promoted to Political Officer of the *county,* and we can leave this backward village forever!"

"By then we'll have anything we want," the woman said cheekily.

Goat Face stuffed the soybeans into his mouth and crunched on them loudly. Tiny bits flew from his mouth. "Why do you think I spend so much time reciting Chairman Mao's teachings? I need to show them I'm not just another country mud ball!" He waved his hand. "Now, get rid of this cheap liquor and bring out that bottle of máo tái

I've been saving. The militia leaders should be here soon!"

A short time later, a tractor chugged noisily down the road and ground to a clattering halt in front of the Political Officer's gate. Goat Face and his wife rushed out to greet their visitors.

The door to the house across the street was ajar. A thin strip of the neighbor's face was visible. He held eye contact briefly with Goat Face, then quickly shut the door. A dog growled inside.

Two men in faded military jackets and red armbands climbed awkwardly off the tractor. The Political Officer helped them unload a wooden box. Together, they hauled it inside. When the militia leaders saw Shí, they couldn't conceal their excitement. The tall one with the bald head and jagged teeth thumped on Shí's chest. His short companion, whose stomach hung heavily over his belt, inspected Shí's face and compared his height to the soldier's.

"I can't believe it's so big!" Chubby exclaimed. "We could sell it and buy a jeep and travel in style!"

Baldy grinned and patted the Political Officer's back. "I wasn't sure what to expect, but you have my full attention now. Is this really from Emperor Qin's tomb?"

Goat Face laughed excitedly. “Who cares where it’s from? I can sell it for a good price and make us all rich!”

His wife ushered the men to the table. “Sit—please! Eat while the food is still hot!”

Bustling about, she loaded the table with plates of sizzling pan-fried pork dumplings, aromatic green-onion pancakes, juicy roasted ribs, crisp stir-fried bean sprouts, and more.

Baldy raised his cup. “To dear Chairman Mao . . . and to our fortunes!”

“To our success!” The Political Officer clinked cups with his guests.

Shí stood motionless by the door and watched the men as they ate and drank. How he wanted to knock their heads together and take the food back to his hungry friend. He resisted, remembering the steep price he had paid for his last impulsive action.

After taking yet another deep swig, Chubby put down his cup. “Should we be drinking this much if we’re going out tonight?”

“Haven’t you heard? Courage flows from the bottle!” Goat Face grinned and emptied his cup.

“We still have plenty of time.” Baldy glanced at his

watch. "I told our men to meet us at the well after midnight."

"Oh, you're so paranoid! We could start earlier. Drink up, drink up," Goat Face urged.

"I'm done. Since you are not going down the hole with us, you finish it." Chubby pushed the bottle closer to Goat Face. "Are you sure we can get away with this?" he asked.

Goat Face refilled his cup and put a chicken drumstick into Chubby's bowl.

"You worry too much, brother! I have this all planned. I promise I will do my part. As soon as Old Chen returns, I'll bring him to meet you. No doubt by then you will have unearthed enough treasure to make us all rich for three lifetimes! Plus, after we blow up the tomb, nobody will know that we were even there."

"I hope you're right," Baldy replied nervously. "You know that the central government has decreed the death penalty for anyone who robs Emperor Qin's tomb."

Goat Face grinned. "Which is exactly why we need *Chen* to take the blame. I announced to the villagers today that he's been stealing treasures. Those fools wouldn't dare question me."

"You crafty fox!" Chubby snickered.

Goat Face lowered his voice. "Now, here's the best part: I've found a way to keep others from capitalizing on our fortune. My cousin down south says that he can sell whatever we find for a good price. That way we can keep the wealth among us. Who's going to report us—the village mud balls? Ha! They're terrified of me!"

"Excellent!" Chubby bent over and popped the top off the wooden box. "This dynamite will make our job much easier."

"Are you sure it will work?" Goat Face asked.

Baldy looked at Chubby and chuckled. "Do you think the neighbors would mind if we gave a demonstration?"

Goat Face stood, swaying unsteadily, his face red from the alcohol. "Of course not! I own this town! If I stamp my foot, I can bring down the rafters of all the houses in Red Star. Follow me!" He grabbed one of the red sticks of dynamite and led the others into the courtyard. His wife hurried excitedly after them.

Through the window, Shí could see the four figures milling around a tree stump in the fading gray daylight. A moment later, they all hurried to one side of the yard. A loud boom rattled the house. Bits of tree, dirt, and bark spewed into the sky. Chickens in the courtyard fluttered and squawked loudly. In the distance, dogs yelped. The men laughed so hard that they started choking, and the woman was doubled over.

Shí had never seen a stick that could make a sound so loud and send so much stuff into the air. He couldn't wait to ask Ming about it.

The group returned. The men plopped down in the armchairs, talking excitedly, while the woman cleared away the dishes.

"You know, our dear Chairman admires Emperor Qin's exploits," said Baldy.

"I love our Chairman's speech about how he outdid Qin Shi Huang's attack against intellectuals," Chubby replied. "What was it he said? Something like, 'Emperor Qin buried four hundred and sixty scholars alive; we have buried forty-six thousand scholars . . . You intellectuals revile us for being Qin Shi Huangs. You are wrong. We have surpassed Qin Shi Huang a hundredfold.'"

Baldy and Goat Face clapped and cheered loudly.

"Well done! Well done, indeed! That is why you are the Communist Party leader of the county militia! No one else has such a memory for our leader's teachings as you." Goat Face laughed dryly.

Chubby nodded with a grin. "Chairman Mao was right—the Emperor was too lenient!"

"Our Chairman is a Qin-Marxist, truly a formidable combination!" said the Political Officer. He was glad he had learned the new phrase "Qin-Marxist" from the radio in time to show it off. Even though he wasn't sure what it meant, he thought it sounded impressive.

Chubby clapped Goat Face on the back in approval. "You, too, are a loyal student of our Chairman!"

The Political Officer's wife brought out a plate of sliced mango, a rare treat, then excused herself, leaving the men to further congratulate one another on their cleverness and their masterful planning.

Eventually, their talking lapsed into heavy snoring that sounded like rusty saws slicing through bricks. When Shí was certain that they were all fast asleep, he walked quietly across the room to the pantry and filled an empty rice sack with food. At the bottom of the pantry he spotted a cardboard box. Curious, he opened it and saw a thick ginseng root.

Shí stuffed the box into the bag and walked out into the dark.

11
FEEDING MING

MING WAS STANDING IN A DIMLY LIT HOUSE. A delicious-smelling white mist danced in front of him. He followed it into the next room, where a large table was piled high with shrimp dumplings, garlic beef, eggs stewed in five-spice tea sauce, glutinous rice wrapped in reed leaves, crispy golden brown spring rolls, and sweet rice cakes decorated with colorful rose petals. Mother was sitting at the head of the table. She held a dumpling between her chopsticks and was smiling warmly at him.

She was saying something, but her words were drowned out by a heavy thumping.

Slowly Ming opened his eyes. The thumping turned to a throbbing pain behind his swollen left lid. He wasn't sure how long he'd been lying on the dirt floor outside the bedroom. Thin strips of moonlight poured through the dirty window, throwing a ghostly pale glow onto the floor next to his face. The pain of his bruised face pressing against the cold floor forced him back to reality.

Eventually, he mustered the strength to push himself upright using the wall. The pounding in his head worsened. His mouth was as dry as dust. Ming saw a chipped enamel cup resting on the floor next to the bed. The mere thought of reaching for it exhausted him. He closed his eyes, trying to will the pain and hunger away. He must have dozed off, because when he opened his eyes again, the moonlight had shifted. He now sat in shadow.

With a gasp, Ming remembered the danger his bā ba was facing and what had happened to his new friend, Shí. His head was awhirl with the events of the afternoon. Legs quivering, he rose unsteadily to his feet. The living room swam before his eyes. Like a blind man, he felt along the wall until his fingers touched the light switch next to the door frame. He flipped on the only light in the room, a naked 25-watt bulb.

"Ming, are you all right?"

A bulky silhouette filled the doorway.

"Shí!"

The soldier rushed over, righted a chair, and helped Ming sit down.

"Are you hurt?" Shí turned Ming's head gently and examined his face.

"It's nothing!" Ming twisted his head away. "I—I—I thought Goat Face took you! How did you escape? Did anyone follow you? What're you—" Nostrils flaring, he squinted at the bag cradled in Shí's arms. "Is that . . . is that . . . *food*?"

Shí grinned proudly and dropped the rice sack onto the desk.

"L-l-let me ha-ha-have it!" Ming's teeth chattered like a hungry horse. His hands stretched eagerly toward the sack.

Shí picked up a wooden bowl from the floor and shook a few crispy dumplings, jiǎo zi, 饺子, into it. "Eat these while I cook up the rest. As we used to say in the Qin army, no soldier can fight on an empty stomach."

Ming's hands trembled as he held the bowl. Tears of gratitude welled up in his eyes.

He bit into a dumpling. A burst of pleasure exploded in his mouth. The meat dumplings had been pan-fried to perfection. They were crispy on the outside, soft and juicy on the inside. Barely pausing to chew, he wolfed them down. His stomach gurgled like an excited frog. Clutching the empty bowl, he followed Shí's movements greedily.

"I found something else that will enhance your vital energy, yuán qì, 元气!" Shí said proudly as he took out the silk-lined box.

"That was for my mother!" Ming exclaimed. "But it arrived too late." His face clouded over. "Father had to give it as a 'present' to the Political Officer."

Ming took the box from Shí's outstretched hands and opened it carefully, making sure the precious ginseng was still inside. He stared at it for a long moment and then gently closed the lid. Ignoring Shí's curious look, he hid the box under a stack of papers on the desk.

"It's fine with me if you want to save it. We have enough food for you now!" said the soldier.

Shí stirred the embers in the stove and threw in a few pieces of coal. Then he set a handless wok on the stove.

While the oil was heating, he chopped up garlic, ginger, and daikon radishes from the bag and tossed them into the wok. Soon a tantalizing aroma filled the room, sending Ming into a frenzy of anticipation.

Ming admired his friend's graceful movements around the stove, not something he would expect from a terra-cotta soldier. The last time he'd tried to cook a meal, he had burned the scallion pancakes into briquettes, and had put so much salt into the soup that his ba ba joked they could use it to kill ants. After that, Bā ba hadn't allowed him to endanger their precious food.

Shí skillfully cracked four eggs into the wok and talked over the sizzling sound. "Your Political Officer and his friends expected me to stand there patiently while they slept off their 'celebration.'" He chuckled and reached into the bag.

"Ming!" Shí pointed at the wall behind Ming. "What's that?"

Turning his head, Ming saw the portrait of Mao grinning benevolently at him. "Oh, that's Chairman Mao." He looked back and caught Shí tossing a handful of something into the wok.

"Hmm. I thought I saw a rat in the corner. I must have

been mistaken," Shí said with a sly smile. He poured in a few drops of soy sauce while briskly stir-frying the ingredients with a spatula.

"What did you just put in?" Ming asked suspiciously.

"Something to make you strong!"

Ming narrowed his eyes as Shí poured the noodle mixture into a large bowl and covered it with the pan-fried eggs. The smell intensified Ming's hunger. Bowing his head in a gesture of thanks, Ming took the bowl. He slurped down a mouthful of noodles. *Delicious!*

He was conscious that Shí was watching him, smiling happily, just as his bā ba would after cooking him a big meal. Shí was right; no soldier could fight on an empty stomach. The food was not only giving Ming strength but lessening the pain in his head too. He could now think straight. He knew that Goat Face would be back looking for Shí, but he decided to deal with it after his stomach was full.

The egg whites were delicately crispy, with the yolks still soft, bursting with sweet, sour, salty, and spicy flavors. The chopped daikon gave the flavorful noodles a satisfying crunch. There was something else in the food that Ming couldn't identify, but as much as he hated to admit it, whatever it was made the dish even tastier than anything his mother had ever cooked.

"What's this?" Ming asked. He held up what looked like a short pink noodle in his chopsticks. "It's delicious! I've never eaten anything quite like it." He tossed it into his mouth.

Shí smiled broadly. "Do you know what Qin soldiers ate when the supply lines were cut? Rats, boiled leather belts, and worms."

Ming hastily put down his empty bowl. "What? You just fed me worms?"

Worm noodles, similar to what Shí served to Ming.

"Yes! Weren't they tasty? I dug them up on the way here. After not eating for so long, you need them to replenish your energy and restore your Chi. Besides, worms are easy to digest."

As hungry as he often was, Ming had never dreamed of eating worms. But Shí was right—they were tasty.

Ming wasn't full yet. He tried to think of a polite way to ask Shí what else was in the bag, when the soldier fished out two bread rolls. He cut them neatly in half, filled them with sliced meat and onions, and handed them to Ming.

"Did Liang teach you how to cook like this?" Ming took a bite.

Shí laughed. "Not exactly. Liang's expertise was limited to helmet stew. I perfected my cooking in the cavalry. Stuffed bread rolls are one of the best ideas we stole from the Mongols. As they spent most of their lives on the move, they would wrap meat in bread and eat with their hands—much easier than eating stir-fried noodles with chopsticks."

"It's so flavorful!" Ming took another greedy bite, closing his eyes in ecstasy. "Thank you!"

He opened his eyes and smiled gratefully at his new friend. "It's been a long time since I ate something this good. So, Shí, how did you get into the cavalry?"

12
JOINING THE CAVALRY

"NOT EASILY." SHÍ SAT DOWN ON THE FLOOR, FACing Ming.

Remember how I had made a vow to join the cavalry when they waved the heads at us? My determination grew over time. Finally, my opportunity came when the frozen ground began to thaw and the black dirt oozed with moisture below the sunny side of the wall. As the Great Wall extended, more soldiers were needed in the cavalry to guard supply lines and depots. I volunteered immediately, but the commander rejected my request, saying that I was too young to fight in a head-on battle. I was heartbroken.

That spring was unusually wet. It rained nonstop for weeks at a time. One morning, during a break in the weather, I spotted a Mongol force riding toward a neighboring tower. We couldn't light the wet straw to send out the warning signal. I ran down to the stable, jumped on a horse, and raced off to the next tower to alert them. Halfway there, the storm resumed, pelting my face like pebbles.

Ming pictured Shí racing through sheets of rain, droplets of water flying off his armor.

When the cavalry commander learned that I had outridden the Mongols to alert our troops, he accepted my transfer request. For the next three months, I practiced fighting with spears and swords on a charging horse. Most important, I learned to fight as part of a team, charging as a single unit while protecting one another.

I was assigned to a unit that guarded a supply depot for the Great Wall in the western Gansu Province. Huge wooden warehouses nestled against the mountainside. They contained materials and supplies collected from all

An early-fourteenth-century watercolor of mounted warriors pursuing enemies, believed to be Mongols.

over China—timber, tools, winter clothes, grain, sorghum wine, dried meat, and wheat. I told myself I was guarding food for my father, but, in truth, I hadn't heard from him or my mother since leaving home six months earlier.

One night, after a long day of drills, I was leading my horse into the stable, when someone slapped me on the back so hard that I almost fell into a pile of hay.

"Wha—?" I turned angrily, fists raised.

There was a loud laugh. "I knew we would not be separated for long!"

"Feng!" I cried joyfully, lowering my fists. "How did you get into the cavalry?"

"You don't think you're the only one who can ride a horse, do you?" Feng asked with a wink.

He pulled two bread rolls stuffed with meat out of his bag. "I 'liberated' these from the quartermaster when he wasn't looking," he whispered conspiratorially. "Come!"

I followed him behind the stables, where we talked and ate under the twinkling stars.

"Did you ever capture a Mongol head?" Ming asked eagerly, stuffing the last bit of bread roll in his mouth.

"Not right away. Our depot was located at the mouth of a canyon. The Mongols could never get past our archers' hail of arrows or our fierce infantry, so we—the cavalry—nestled in tents set among the warehouses, getting fat and lazy. I grew frustrated."

Feng was an optimist and assured me we would get our chance. But he was wrong. The Mongols gave up attacking the depot. Instead, they began to raid our supply caravans. We had to divide our forces.

By this time, both Feng and I were dying to get out of the camp. We volunteered to escort a caravan transporting rice, tools, and herbal medicine to a new section of the

Great Wall. The morning our unit left, icy snow bit at our faces, and a stiff wind cut through our cotton jackets like knives. At noon, when we stopped for lunch, Feng brought me warm ginger soup in his helmet.

"Hurry!" he said. "Drink it quickly so you can sneak back into line for more."

I slurped down the hot broth as quickly as I could while he gnawed on a half-frozen bread roll. When I finished, I took our helmets to get us more soup while he went for noodles.

We were a great team.

Ming wished that he had a friend like Feng. He would have shared everything with him, as he had with his friends in Xi'an. Soon after moving to Red Star, he had started a conversation with a classmate. At first, the boy, whose name was Yang, seemed shy, but when Ming told him that he was building a radio, Yang became very talkative and friendly, showing great interest.

Ming was excited and planned to invite Yang over that weekend. But when he talked to the boy the next day, Teacher Panda pointed at Yang and called out, "Why are you talking to the bourgeois boy?"

Since then, whenever they met, Yang would look around nervously and quickly walk away.

After lunch, we entered a valley. The wind whistled through the trees and rattled the barren branches around us. When we reached a sloping hill, Mongols charged down from behind the tree line. We immediately moved into a circular defensive formation around our supplies, facing outward.

The enemy's fierce attack and their loud drums startled our horses. Two of my brothers-in-arms were bucked off their horses. One broke his neck in the fall and was trampled by his own horse; the other was dragged off by the enemy. Fear drowned out any excitement I had felt before. We would have been wiped out if a regular patrol had not come to our aid. Humiliated, we stumbled back to camp, clothes torn and covered in blood, carrying our wounded and dragging our dead.

Unlike those lucky cavalrymen who guarded the Great Wall and could see the Mongols from far away, we were fighting shadows and chasing ghosts. Once we left the camp, we never knew when we would fall into an ambush. During battles, I tried to stay at the center of our formation,

away from the enemy. Unfortunately, being a coward didn't give me a chance to kill any Mongols.

"What about your shield and pine-tree jacket?" Ming asked quietly. "I thought that was supposed to keep you safe!"

"Ah, you remembered that! Well, by then I had outgrown the jacket. And . . . I lost it."

"How could you lose it?" Ming asked angrily. He thought about the last sweater his mother had sewn for him. It was too small now, but he still kept it at the bottom of the wooden chest under his bed.

Shí avoided Ming's gaze. "I was trying to stay alive. The long winter was hard on us. Many fell ill, and our horses, bred for a warmer climate, were unable to compete with those of the Mongols in the bitter cold. During one of their ambushes, the Mongols seized my gear, including the jacket."

"That's awful!" Ming let out a sympathetic sigh.

I had nightmares every night. The young Mongol I had killed on the wall kept haunting me. The boy's face was so vivid and his cry so clear. Other times I dreamed that my

father had fallen ill on the wall and that my mother, weeping, stood in the road holding an empty rice jar. I was afraid to close my eyes.

One night I woke Feng with my cries. When he asked me what was wrong, I was too ashamed to speak. How could I claim that I loved my family while hiding like a coward? I swore that I would fight with honor and face the Mongols like a man.

"So did the Mongols kill you?" Ming asked.

A scowl fell over Shí's face, and his gaze hardened. Ming wondered if the soldier was tempted to smack him for asking such a rude question. He quickly changed the subject.

"Um . . . uh . . . so what exactly happened at the Political Officer's house this afternoon?"

Shí's face regained its composure. "Oh, his friends brought him a box of sticks called dy-no-mite." He struggled with the unfamiliar word. "They plan to use them to break into the Emperor's tomb."

A chill ran down Ming's spine. His back stiffened. "Why didn't you tell me sooner?"

"Bah! There is nothing to worry about. I watched one

go off." Shí scoffed. "It is only good for scaring chickens and dogs. It won't even scratch the Emperor's tomb."

Ming stood up, spreading his arms to emphasize his point. "Shí! One stick might not do much, but bundled together, they can cause massive destruction!"

"Relax, Ming! The tomb is stronger than rock. Do you know that during its construction, workers shot arrows at the walls? If they left any marks, the structure was taken down and rebuilt."

"Trust me, Shí. Those sticks can do a lot more damage than your sticks with pointy heads. Dynamite can blow a tunnel through a mountain. You have to warn your friends!"

Ming realized what he'd just said. If Shí left to warn his friends, what was going to happen to him and his bā ba?

"Ah . . . perhaps I should," Shí replied. "The men are planning to break in through the well where I was found. They also talked about framing someone else for robbing the tomb."

"Who?"

"Someone named Old Chen."

The color drained from Ming's face. "Shí, that's . . . that's my bā ba!" His mind raced, and the words came tumbling out. “He should be back by now. I wish I knew where he was. But if we warn your friends and stop the raid, we can protect the tomb. Then there won’t be anything for them to accuse my father of, right?”

“I suppose so,” Shí said thoughtfully. “In that case, we must go into the tomb.”

“But you just said they’ll be at the well. How are we going to get past them?”

“If you can guide me to the west side of Li Mountain. I know of a secret entrance.”

“A secret entrance?” Ming cried.

“Yes. It was meant for the Emperor’s chief consul, Li Si. Emperor Qin planned to run the country from his tomb. Li Si was supposed to visit the mausoleum and make regular reports, but he never came.”

Ming thought that some other time he should tell Shí that Li Si had been killed by his political adversary soon after the Emperor’s death, and how, shortly after that, a peasants’ uprising had overthrown the dynasty.

Ming opened the desk drawer and fished out a flashlight. “All right, let’s go! I know a back road out of the village.” As he grabbed his jacket, he remembered the stories he had heard at the teahouse. “Are there really traps in the tomb?” he asked.

“Of course!”

“How will we get past them?”

“If you follow my instructions, I can get you through. My only fear is General Wang.”

“Who is he?”

“I'll tell you later. Hurry!”

13
CHENGFU BATTLE

A THICK LAYER OF SNOW NOW CARPETED THE VILlage, blanketing the signs of early spring. The vast white landscape resembled unpainted white silk, colorless and vague. The moon and stars cast stark, cold light over Red Star.

Ming led the way. As if they were crossing a frozen lake, he and Shí trod carefully along the road, stopping with calculated abruptness and turning quickly to make sure they weren't being followed. They hugged the walls, pausing every now and then in the shadows between houses to listen. But the only sound was the low crackling of stoves warming the houses. Dark coal smoke rose from rooftops into the clear sky.

The road took them to the edge of an open field. Ming breathed deeply and savored the feel of cold air on his bruised face.

"That's the way to Li Mountain," he whispered, pointing at a narrow path branching off the main road and leading up the mountain.

Shí set off, taking huge strides like a prowling tiger. Ming picked his way around the jutting stones of the steep path, panting as he tried to keep up.

Contemporary view of Li Mountain in summer.

Shí stopped abruptly. "Are you sure this is right? I remember Li Mountain being a lot taller."

Ming shrugged. "Bā ba said that after the government gave the order to chop down the trees on the mountain to build houses in the cities, nothing was left to stop the soil from being swept away by the wind and rain. It's turned the Wei River brown." As he turned to point to the river below, he slipped on a wet stone.

"Be careful!" Shí caught Ming's arm. "Here, let me carry you."

Ming shrugged off Shí's grasp, blushing. "I'm fine. I just need to watch where I step!"

Shí got down on one knee. "Come on, Ming. I can't find the entrance if you break your neck."

Reluctantly, Ming climbed onto Shí's back. He wrapped his arms around Shí's broad shoulders, the way he used to with his bā ba.

Shí stood up slowly, supporting Ming's legs with his arms.

Like tea leaves in hot water, memories unfurled before Ming. When he was young, his bā ba had carried him around Xi'an on his back, telling him stories of ancient times.

"We must find two large boulders leaning against each other on the west side of the mountain," said Shí.

"Oh, you mean the Camel's Humps. That's where my class went to hunt birds." Ming grimaced at the memory. "Keep going straight." He pointed ahead. "Now can you tell me about General Wang?"

"Ah, the One-Armed General!"

"How did he lose his arm?"

"He cut it off himself!"

"What?"

"For it to make sense, I have to tell you about the battle. Remember how I told you that China was divided into seven states before Emperor Qin?"

"Yes. And he conquered them all!" Ming answered.

"That's correct! The Emperor was a brilliant commander. He spent years studying Sun Tzu's *The Art of War*. However, even the Emperor made mistakes, and none worse than when he launched an attack against the state of Chu."

"I've heard of Chengfu Battle!" Ming waved one of his arms excitedly. "The old men at the teahouse love to talk about it! Emperor Qin was expecting a quick victory, but his army fell into a trap!"

"That's right. Back then, General Wang was only a lowly lieutenant in the shock troops—the infantrymen who led attacks against the enemy. At that particular battle, the commanding officer ordered the army into the awl, zhuī zi, 锥子, a formation shaped like a needle. The shock troops, led by Lieutenant Wang at the tip, would punch through the enemy. Archers behind would shoot to the rear of the enemy ranks, while cavalry charged to break up their defenses.

"The men in the shock troop were famous for fighting fiercely—like cornered tigers. They were the largest and strongest men in the Qin army. It was rumored that some had studied *jiao li* under the Emperor's wrestling masters."

"What's *jiao li*?"

"Do you know about martial arts?"

"Like kung fu?" Ming punched his fist in the air to demonstrate.

"It's similar." Shí bounced Ming up on his back.

"The shock troops were handpicked for their strength and aggression. They fought with great courage and determination and were well rewarded for their bravery. A poor peasant could gain land, fame, and fortune, all in a single battle."

These days, Ming thought bitterly, you didn't need strength or courage. To live well, you just needed to be from the working class and join the Communist Party. Some days he wished his bā ba was a farmer or factory worker.

To everyone's surprise, the Emperor's army met only light resistance as it marched toward the city of Chengfu. A random volley of arrows here and there, or a quick attack from small forces of skirmishers who then retreated. As they approached the narrow canyon leading to the city gates, soldiers were joking that the enemy was busy preparing a banquet welcoming the Qin army.

When the last of the archers had entered the canyon, a whistling suddenly filled the air, and the sparrows scattered from the trees. As enemy arrows rained down, the shock troops whipped their shields over their heads, creating a turtle-shaped defensive formation. When the onslaught stopped, dead birds and arrows were pinned to their shields, sticking out like porcupine needles.

Ming thought about the old men at the teahouse munching on peanuts while criticizing the Emperor's strategies, as if they were all great military analysts. Sometimes their intense arguments almost reached the point of a fistfight, but none of their stories were as vivid and exciting as what Shí was describing to him now.

Just as the infantry emerged from under their shields, a rushing sound filled the canyon. The soldiers looked around in confusion before realizing that huge cauldrons of burning oil were racing down the steep cliffs. As the scalding waves engulfed the Qin forces, the shrieking of dying horses drowned out the terrified screams of the soldiers. Half of Lieutenant Wang's men were on the ground, some drowning facedown in puddles of black, steaming oil.

Knowing that another attack would wipe out the rest of his squad, Lieutenant Wang led his men on a charge toward Chengfu. "Follow me!" he cried. "Long live Emperor Qin!"

As they approached the city gates, the doors were thrown open. Chu cavalry burst out and surrounded them.

The mountain path ended at a crossroads. Shí paused, and Ming flicked on the flashlight. Shí raised his eyebrows at the circle of light.

"Oh! A small lantern. Another new invention!"

"Well, sort of. Turn left here."

Shí turned onto an even steeper path.

A thick mist hung above the treetops, softening the moonlight to a dim yellow glow. Bare tree branches brushed Ming's shoulders. Occasionally, a cry and caw broke the stillness as ravens made themselves heard.

"So, what happened to General Wang?" Ming asked.

Realizing that his troops would never stand a chance cowering together like frightened sheep, General Wang called out, "For Emperor Qin!"

Like a man possessed, he led his squad charging directly into the enemy cavalry, hacking wildly. The soldier beside him took a spear in the face, leaving Wang's flank exposed. A large horseman rode up and swung his sword in a long arc, cutting deeply into Wang's left arm, leaving it dangling by only a thin strip of flesh and tendon.

After the battle, the tale quickly spread that Wang, without hesitation, had thrown himself to the ground to avoid the horseman's second swing. Gritting his teeth, he severed his own arm. To stop the bleeding, he pressed a handful of dirt onto the stump.

Flinching, Ming remembered roaring in agony after slicing open a finger while cleaning a broken clay bowl. The throbbing pain from the small wound had lasted for days.

The horseman, who had wheeled around to finish the lieutenant off, faltered in disbelief. Screaming like an enraged hawk, Wang picked up his sword with his remaining hand, leaped up, and slashed his attacker's thigh to the bone. The rider fell to the ground and was crushed beneath the hooves of his own horse.

At this point, most men would have fainted from blood loss or shock, but Lieutenant Wang fought on. Inspired by his bravery, his men broke free and retreated through the canyon back to Xi'anyang.

When the story reached Emperor Qin, he promoted Wang to general. Later that year, General Wang returned with an army of six hundred thousand men and conquered Chu.

Ming had heard many stories of revolutionary heroes, but none were this exciting. He wondered: If General

Wang were still alive, would Chairman Mao make him a national hero?

"Every Qin soldier knew that the One-Armed General's actions earned the Emperor's army a fearless reputation."

"Wow! Did you fight under General Wang to conquer Chu?"

"No. By the time I joined, China was already unified. However, I fought my last battle under his command."

"Your last battle? What happened?"

"We are here," Shí grunted. The soldier abruptly loosened his grip. Ming tumbled off, landing unsteadily on the rough ground.

"Ouch!"

14
JOURNEY TO THE TOMB

THE MIST PARTED, ALLOWING THE MOON TO ILLUMINATE the valley. Ming looked at what the villagers called the Camel's Humps—two enormous boulders shaped like large haystacks, propped against each other below the mountain's peak.

Ming had been here before but never suspected that there could be a secret entrance. "Where is it?"

Shí ignored Ming's question. He dropped to his knees in front of where the boulders met and separated the bushes. "Someone has broken in!" he exclaimed. "The entrance should be sealed!"

"Huh? Where?" Ming hurried over and saw an opening the size of a wheelbarrow between the two boulders. He didn't remember seeing it on his class trip. He shone the flashlight into the hole.

"Did someone beat us here?" Shí lowered his voice. "Now, stay alert and follow me!" With that, he turned and crawled inside.

Ming followed tentatively on his hands and knees. The ground was damp and soft. Once inside, he stood and shone the flashlight around. The still air reeked of decay and mold.

They were in a cave about the size of his family's courtyard. Moss hung from the ceiling, and moonlight filtered through a small hole high above them. In a far corner was a stone door, half hidden behind thick vegetation. Ming took a tentative step—and immediately tripped on something.

"Āī yo!" he yelped. Shining his flashlight around, he saw that he had stepped on an oil lamp. He looked at Shí. "How'd *that* get here?"

Shí picked it up. "It must belong to whoever left the entrance open. There is oil still in it. Can you light it?"

Cradling the flashlight between his neck and shoulder, Ming fished out the box of matches from his jacket. He opened the glass shutter and deftly lit the lamp's wick. Shí placed it in the center of the cave. Ming stuffed the flashlight into his breast pocket.

"Whoa . . ." Ming stared at the stone door. It was intricately carved with a dragon, lóng, 龙, and phoenix, fèng, 凤. A glint caught his gaze. "Is that . . . is that jade?"

In the center of the door, a green ball the size of his fist was resting in the jaws of the menacing dragon. The ball had a hint of red at its core.

"Yes," Shí answered proudly.

Ming moved closer. The ball glowed with a dreamy pinkish green light. He reached for it.

Shí suddenly pushed him on the shoulder, shoving him out of the way. Startled, Ming fell to the ground. He yelped as his knee cracked against something hard. Grimacing, he saw that he had landed on a small bronze frog, one of three that were nesting among the moss.

"Are you always so careless?" Shí huffed. "Did you not see the dragon's eyes?"

Ming looked up. "What? I see . . . cobwebs in its hollow eyes."

"There are more than cobwebs there, my young friend. If you touch that jade ball, Emperor Qin will welcome you with arrows."

"Yeah—as if they're still going to work after thousands of years." Ming let out a nervous laugh. He stood up, brushing a few dead leaves off his pants.

Shí gestured over his shoulder with his thumb. "Why don't you ask him? I think that's where your lamp came from."

Ming looked where Shí was pointing. With a moan, he sank back down to the floor. Fear rippled down his spine. Opposite the door and leaning against the wall was the shriveled corpse of a man wrapped in a Mao-style jacket. Some frozen flesh still hung from his frame. Two thin, long arrows protruded from the shrunken sockets where his eyes had once been. His mouth was wide open, as if he were still amazed by the beauty of the jade ball. His tongue protruded obscenely, like a twisted slug.

Shí gripped Ming's arm and pulled him to his feet. "Those arrows were *his* reward!"

Ming shivered when he saw a tattered purple patch on

the elbow of the dead man's jacket. He had seen it before. The jacket belonged to the fourth Gee brother—the one who had gone missing a few months ago. That purple patch had become famous in the village after the Political Officer had criticized him for the gaudy, bourgeois color. The man had refused to take it off because his wife had sewn it on before dying in childbirth.

Shí was now kneeling in front of the stone door, arms outstretched, hands placed on the two outer frogs. His head rested on the center one, the one Ming had tripped over.

"What are you doing?"

"Anyone who wishes to enter the Emperor's tomb must show the proper respect." Shí sat back on his heels, staring intently at the middle frog.

Ming was stunned when Shí suddenly grabbed its head and twisted. With a faint click, the head came off.

The stone door began to swing inward. The low, metallic screech of the ancient hinges made the roots of Ming's teeth ache. He stepped aside, worried that arrows might shoot at him or a squad of terra-cotta soldiers might dash out to crush him.

A faint breeze stirred, and the delicate aroma of sandalwood, incense, and herbal medicine caressed him like warm water.

"Ah! It worked!" Shí exclaimed. "Just as my brothers who maintain the door told me!" He examined the walnut-size frog's head in his rough palm. "This was the key for Li Si to enter the tomb." He rose to his feet, gently cupping the frog's head in both hands.

Ming stuffed the flashlight into his pocket, picked up the oil lamp, and followed Shí down a narrow stone tunnel. His shirt clung wetly to his back, and his breath came in short gasps.

Behind them, the door closed with a low rumble. Red lanterns above immediately flared to life.

"Whoa!" Ming jumped in surprise and dropped the lamp. He shielded his eyes from the unexpected light. "Did we just set off the alarm?" Frightening stories from the teahouse flashed through his mind.

Shí picked up the lamp and set it against the wall. "No, don't worry. To save whale oil, these lanterns are lit only when someone enters. They were meant for the court officials who never came."

Ming looked around eagerly as they walked down the tunnel. The walls were carved with extravagant scenes and landscapes: mountains, rivers, and heavenly clouds, and bridges and roads that looped through tree-filled parks. People were flying colorful kites and boating across lakes. Every scene was vividly colored, highlighted in red, gold, and silver.

The tunnel led them to a garden larger than Ming's school yard. White half circles of stone paved the ground. Shí stopped next to a large pond in the center of the garden. With a flourish, he swept his hand around. "Welcome to the mausoleum of Emperor Qin!"

The red lanterns gave off a soft glow tinged with a touch of yellow, like moonlight. A giant bas-relief portrait spanned the full length of the wall beyond the pond. A stern-looking man in a golden robe stood atop a mountain, encircled by a continuous array of dragons and phoenixes.

The ornate gold ceiling was carved with the figures of peacocks—the symbol of authority, intelligence, and virtue—and phoenixes—the symbol of beauty and femininity. They were arranged in a pattern around the Ball of Harmony—a symbol of unity and infinity.

Ming's eyes were hungry for every detail. After years of hearing tales and daydreaming about the tomb's splendor and magnificence, he was now able to see it and compare myth with reality. His heart danced with joy, but at the same time he felt a pang of sadness. How he wished his bā ba were there with him!

He couldn't help but reach out and brush his hands lightly over the green lotus leaves, which were covered with networks of tender veins. They floated in the pond among pink flowers and goldfish with colorful scales sparkling with silver and gold. Upon closer inspection, he realized the silk leaves were thicker and less glossy than the real ones in the village pond. He reached down and felt the cool porcelain scales of the fish.

Shí pushed aside overlapping lotus leaves. "Help me find the headless frog."

Ming searched among the leaves and flowers. He saw bronze frogs in various poses hidden among the plants. One was in mid-leap, supported by a thin metal rod as it hopped over to a nearby pink petal. Another, beneath a large leaf against the bank of the pond, had its short front legs lifted into the air, showing the intricate webbing between its toes, as if it were trying to hop. It had no head.

"I found it!" Ming exclaimed.

Shí bent over and placed the head from the cave frog

Frog among lotus leaves and flowers.

onto its body. There was a soft clicking sound. "There! Now the alarm is disabled." He stood up.

"But—but how are we going to get out?" Ming tried to mask the fear in his voice.

"Just remove the head and retrace our path. But don't forget to return the head at the entrance!"

With that, Shí turned and marched off.

15
INSIDE THE TOMB

MING TRIED TO KEEP UP WITH SHÍ WHILE TAKING IN his surroundings. In the center of each white marble slab lining the floor was the character for one of the five elements. Each symbol had its own color: wood, mù, 木, blue; fire, huǒ, 火, red; earth, tǔ, 土, yellow; metal, jīn, 金, silver; and water, shuǐ, 水, black.

His eyes struggled to cope with the contrasts of bright colors. Lining the path was a profusion of porcelain and silk flowers—roses, jasmine, and orchids—in shades of red and yellow, purple and pink, lavender and white. There were bowl-size peonies of every imaginable shade. The petals of the Golden Claw chrysanthemums opened like dancers' hands, capturing the soft light shining from the lanterns. It was hard for Ming to believe that none of them were real.

Suddenly, he felt the ground shift slightly beneath his left foot. Ming looked down. He saw that he had stepped on the bottom half of a gold character, Emperor, huáng, 皇. A faint hissing sound escaped from the head of a chrysanthemum.

"Wh-wh-what's happening?"

Shí spun around and swiftly dropped to his knees. He pressed both hands on the upper half of the 皇 just as a metal spike burst from the head of the flower. It froze inches from Ming's neck and then slid back into the chrysanthemum.

The color drained from Ming's face, and his knees shook. Now everything around him seemed to be full of danger.

"Don't *ever* step on 'Emperor'!" Shí said harshly. He got up. In a softer tone, he added, "Sorry. I forgot to warn you. Follow my steps."

"Ah, I'll remember that!" Ming murmured uneasily.

Shí stepped off the curving path and walked among large flower-bearing trees. Ming followed closely. They came to a courtyard that was filled with deep-red roses, hoof-shaped white lilies, and fire-colored mountain tea flowers.

Ming was captivated by the full moon above in the celestial ceiling. It was surrounded by shining, glittering stars. In a far corner of the courtyard was a small bamboo grove. Lifelike porcelain birds and crickets perched here and there among the stalks. Ming would have thought them alive if not for the eerie silence. He wondered if there really were eight thousand clay soldiers guarding the tomb. Where could they be?

On one side of the courtyard was a building with a sloping, pagoda-style roof made out of glazed tiles. On each soaring eave, a dragon led a row of eight small figures from famous legends. Red lacquer pillars flanked the door. Faint light shone through white rice paper over four large intricate latticework windows. In the middle of each window was a black character: bravery, dǎn, 胆; discipline, lǜ, 律; loyalty, zhōng, 忠; and glory, róng, 荣.

Shí took Ming by the wrist and pulled him into the shadows next to the door.

"Where are we? Where is everyone?" Ming whispered.

"The armory. Most soldiers are stationed around the main tomb, deeper inside the mountain," Shí said in a low voice. "No one ever comes here. Guarding the weapons is one of the easiest jobs—as long as you can track numbers and know how to maintain the yellow-powder trap. Si Ji got the job because he knows the mechanics of the trap, but how my friend Feng managed to wiggle himself into the position is beyond me. Stay here!"

Without waiting for Ming's response, Shí walked up the steps and slowly pushed open the door. He stuck his head inside before entering, leaving the door ajar.

Ming crouched among the porcelain, enamel, and bronze flowers. Soon curiosity got the better of him, and he gingerly inched toward the building to look through the door, careful not to touch anything.

Lamplight glittered off rows of iron and bronze swords. Burnished copper shields hung above the weapons, glinting under red lanterns. Ming detected a metallic tang in the air. Shadows moved on the far wall under a yellow flag emblazoned with the character Qín, 秦.

Shí and two other terra-cotta soldiers moved into Ming's view. They stood next to a life-size bronze chariot pulled by four muscular terra-cotta horses. The two soldiers were about Shí's height and of the same gray color. One of them had big ears and had his hair tied into a topknot. The other had a long mustache and a grim, fierce expression.

Unearthed carriage pulled by four terra-cotta horses, from the tomb of Emperor Qin.

"Where have you been, Shí?" asked Long Mustache. "We've been going crazy trying to find you!"

"I was dragged out by some farmers while I was on a ladder, checking the ceiling alarm. They broke me into pieces with their clumsy shovels. It took some effort to restore me."

"So it was you! We heard they had to patch a hole near

the moon gate. What was it like up there?" the big-eared soldier asked excitedly.

"A lot has changed, Feng!" Shí answered.

"Such as?" asked Long Mustache.

"They have a magic box that can talk and sing endlessly! I'll tell you more later, Si Ji. Right now I need to make a report to General Wang. Tomb robbers are coming, and Ming says they have a weapon that can crack open a mountain!"

"Who is Ming?" asked Si Ji.

"A friend who put me back together."

Ming detected a hint of uneasiness in Shí's voice.

"A 'friend'? As in a 'human'?" demanded Si Ji.

Shí's mouth opened a fraction, enough to serve as confirmation.

"You didn't reveal the location of the tomb, did you? If you brought him here, General Wang would cut off his head, just like he did to us"—Feng chopped down his hand—"and then break you into pieces."

Ming jerked his head back from the opening. Maybe coming here was a mistake. How could he explain the threat of dynamite to these terra-cotta soldiers? Would

Shí be able to protect him? And what did Feng mean, "cut off his head just like he did to us"?

"You have to believe me," Shí pleaded. "Ming is not a thief, and the threat is real. I just hope the tomb robbers won't be able to get past the yellow-powder trap."

"There might be . . . a problem," said Si Ji. "We haven't inspected it for a while."

Shí scowled. "How long?"

"Oh . . . maybe three or four hundred years? You know how frustrating it is to work on that mechanism with these big stubby fingers." Feng wiggled his fingers and laughed uneasily.

"But it requires regular maintenance!" Shí sounded angry.

"Have you ever tried removing the wall panels to get to the gears? It takes days!" said Si Ji.

"You lazy pigs!" Shí was furious. "Besides guarding the armory, this trap is your only responsibility! You are putting the Emperor and his tomb at risk!"

Si Ji took a step back. "But no one has tried to break in for two thousand years!"

"And there are other traps too," said Feng defensively.

"Stop pointing your finger at us. What about you, calling a human thief 'friend'!"

Ming's mind spun like a windmill. He could find his way back to the frog . . . maybe. He started to back away, when his bā ba's favorite saying popped into his head: "In order to get a cub, one must dare to enter the tiger's cave."

He was no coward! He couldn't just leave. If the Political Officer blew open the tomb, both Shí and his bā ba would be in danger. He had to find a way to save them.

Ming straightened his shoulders, took a deep breath, and pushed open the door. He envisioned himself as a revolutionary hero right out of the movies, fearless and indomitable.

"We have no time to argue among ourselves," he declared in a loud voice. "We need to check on the trap."

The three terra-cotta soldiers greeted him with stares of disbelief.

Si Ji looked Ming up and down, then turned to Shí. "You *did* bring a human here!"

Shí walked over and placed a hand on Ming's arm. "This is Ming. He is the one who restored me and guided me back. A corrupt official in his village is plotting to break in here to steal the treasures and then blame it on his father."

"Perhaps it's your little *friend* who wants to steal the treasure," Si Ji said.

Ming puffed up his narrow chest indignantly and twisted his lips in revulsion. "I am not a thief! In fact, it is my job—actually, my father's job—to *stop* thieves and protect ancient treasures."

Si Ji squinted at Ming with cool calculation.

Shí pointed at Ming's face. "See that bruise? He earned that while trying to protect me from the real tomb robbers. You should trust him!"

"And I say we should follow the rules and kill this human now." Si Ji looked at Feng for support.

"Ming is about the same age we were when we joined the Emperor's army," Shí said earnestly. "Don't you remember when all we wanted was to save our loved ones?"

"Enough, Si Ji," said Feng. "Shí is right. We need to make sure the yellow-powder trap is working." Feng avoided eye contact with Shí and beckoned for everyone to follow him out into the courtyard.

Si Ji stabbed a finger at Ming. "Stay close. I'm watching you!"

16

THE YELLOW-POWDER TRAP

MING, SHÍ, AND SI JI FOLLOWED FENG ACROSS THE courtyard to the corner of the bamboo grove. They watched closely as Feng reached for a yellow bird perched on one of the stalks. He "flapped" one of its wings. Near them, a section of the wall, about hip height, retracted, revealing a small opening.

Si Ji got on his knees and stuck his head inside. He tried to reach for something, but the narrow opening blocked his broad shoulders.

Shí whispered to Ming, "The gears that control the yellow-powder trap are up there." He pointed to the wall above the opening.

Si Ji pulled out his head and stood up. "The main gear is all corroded. I can't reach it."

Feng sighed. "We should not have waited so long. Now we have to take out all the wall panels."

"But that will take days!" Shí's voice was taut with anxiety. "I bet you don't even know where your tools are."

Ming stepped up to the opening. "May I try?"

"No! Don't let him!" Si Ji exclaimed, blocking the opening with his body. "He's going to break it completely so his tomb-robber friends can get in."

"If he breaks anything, I will strangle him on the spot." Feng pulled Si Ji aside. "Besides, I don't think this little twig is strong enough to strangle a baby bird, let alone damage the trap."

"Ming is good at fixing things," said Shí. "I saw how he fixed a machine." He patted Ming's shoulder. "See if you can make the gear move again. Be careful, though! If you accidentally trip it, the heavy weight will drop down and crush you."

Ming knelt in front of the opening and pulled out his flashlight. He slowly poked his head through and twisted and wriggled his upper body inside. It was a tight squeeze.

He could see a large bellows in front of him. It was attached to a sealed clay urn the size of an oil drum. From the urn ran long brass tubes that disappeared into the wall. Next to the urn was a large gear, which was interlocked with smaller ones.

Ming was surprised by how similar the gear arrangement was to some of the clocks he had fixed. He turned his head and saw that there was a heavy chain attached to the main gear. It ran up and over a pulley. A heavy weight was suspended above him at the end of the chain.

Ming could see that the main gear, when triggered, would turn and send the weight down, compressing the bellows and blowing the powder out of the urn through the tubes. A large knot of corrosion was jammed in between the gear's teeth. When he realized that the only thing holding the weight over his head was a millennia-old chain, he shivered.

"Get me a rag and some oil, please," he called out.

"Feng, watch him," Si Ji said as he stomped off.

Ming reached into his pocket and pulled out his

screwdriver. Slowly he began chipping away at the rust around the chain. Much to his relief, it did not take long before scales of corrosion began breaking loose.

"Be careful!" Shí's voice was full of concern.

Si Ji returned with a bucket of oil and a rag.

Ming stretched out his hand. Si Ji quickly dipped the rag in oil and slapped it into Ming's palm. After dabbing oil on the gears, Ming scraped at the rust with his screwdriver again. More flakes broke loose, and he felt a small movement in the chain.

Ming pulled himself out, and Shí helped him to stand.

"Let's test it," said Ming.

Feng ran over and pressed down on the yellow bird's beak. Nothing happened.

"I knew it! He's a saboteur!" Si Ji exclaimed, reaching for Ming.

With a loud crack, the gears began clattering. Si Ji's arms froze in midair. The bellows started wheezing.

Feng quickly let go of the beak. At once, the noise stopped and the mechanism ground to a halt.

Ming held his breath, looking around nervously. When he was sure that there was no poison powder in the air, he exhaled slowly.

Shí clapped his hands. "He did it! I told you he was not a tomb robber!"

A deep, authoritative voice filled the courtyard. "What is all this talk about tomb robbers?"

17
"YOU HAVE TO BELIEVE US!"

MING TURNED AROUND, HIS EXPRESSION CAUGHT between surprise and fear. As he beheld the large figure before him, the air was sucked out of his lungs and his body involuntarily tensed. A commanding-officer's cap with two long pheasant feathers rested atop the figure's head. His large eyes and thin, slightly hooked nose reminded Ming of an owl. His groomed mustache sat above a mouth with firm lips. Ribbons and studs decorated his full-body stone armor. A long sword, with a carved piece of green jade the size of a duck egg set into its pommel, hung off his left hip. More striking than anything was his distinct lack of a left arm.

In one smooth motion, the three soldiers sank to their knees, pressing their foreheads against the ground. "Long live Emperor Qin!"

Ming couldn't decide if he should drop to his knees like the soldiers.

"Honorable General! I am sorry we disturbed you." Shí's voice quavered. It was the first time that Ming had seen him show fear.

"Rise!" The general's voice sounded as rough as bark.

The soldiers rose as one, heads bowed.

The general pointed at Ming. "Correct me if I am wrong, but he was not buried with us, was he?"

Ming felt his scalp tighten under General Wang's gaze. He allowed his eyes to rest on the general's face for a few moments before focusing on Shí's quivering legs.

"No, sir." Shí's eyes darted to the ground.

"So tell me, how did this tomb robber get in here?" The general addressed Shí in a stern voice.

Ming could feel the beads of perspiration forming on his forehead. His eyes darted from General Wang to Shí.

"H-h-he is Shí's friend, not a tomb robber," Feng stammered. "He brought us news of an im-im-impending attack, and he even helped us to . . . ah . . . fix the yellow-powder trap."

Ming felt a sense of gratitude. Did Feng really believe him now, or was he just protecting his friend Shí? Either way, Ming was encouraged by Feng's support and lifted his chin to meet the general's gaze.

Shí moved in front of Ming, as if shielding him from the general. "It is true. Corrupt officials are planning to break into the tomb using exploding sticks called 'dynamite.'"

General Wang's eyes widened and his jaw slackened. A stubborn, deathly silence settled over the room.

At long last, the general waved his hand dismissively. "Let them come! Many have tried, but this mausoleum has proved to be impregnable." He frowned and addressed Shí. "You have disobeyed me again by bringing this human here. I will make sure you both receive the proper punishment."

Ming took a deep breath and stepped forward. "General, I have seen how dynamite blows through a mountain!" His voice was constricted, as though invisible hands were squeezing his thin throat.

General Wang squinted suspiciously at Ming. It was the sort of look one might give to someone telling a poor lie, a look that mingled pity and disdain. "No one has ever broken in before. Even if they succeed, they won't leave here alive," he said coldly.

"Sir! You have to believe us!" said Shí. "Things outside have changed."

General Wang ignored Shí's plea and addressed Feng and Si Ji. "Lock them up in the storage room and report back to your stations. I will punish them later."

Without giving Shí or Ming another look, General Wang walked out.

18
SHÍ'S LAST BATTLE

YELLOW LANTERNS CAST A GOLDEN GLOW ON THE rows of shelves standing in the middle of the storage room. They were laden with old parchment and small porcelain jars decorated with flowers.

A door on one side of the room had a fan-shaped viewing window with elaborate lattices. Two round porcelain stools flanked the door, each decorated with the character 囍—for "double happiness," xǐ—and never-ending knot patterns.

Ming closed his eyes momentarily, concentrating on

the sound of Feng's and Si Ji's retreating footsteps. He guessed that it must be well past midnight. The events of the previous day played over and over in his mind like the propaganda songs on the radio: meeting Shí . . . having him taken away . . . learning about Goat Face's plan to break into the tomb and frame his bā ba . . . encountering General Wang . . . and, now, being locked up. His plan to stop Goat Face had melted like snow on hot coals.

Exhaustion suddenly washed over him. He thought about being locked in the tomb forever, turning the idea over and over, like sucking on a dry, sour plum.

He looked through the window into a corridor lit by purple lanterns. The walls nearby were decorated with jeweled cherry blossoms. Farther along were elaborately carved fishermen pulling a net from a river. At the end of the corridor were two majestic bronze lions guarding a moon gate—a circular opening. It was framed by scrolls. In large black characters, the left scroll bore the inscription "In Paradise, the days stretch on and on." The right scroll said, "The trees stay green all year long." The one above read, "Heavenly Paradise."

"I'm sorry I brought you here." Shí patted Ming's shoulder.

A moon gate.

"It's not your fault. I wanted to come," Ming replied.

"That's where the farmers dragged me out." Shí pointed toward the moon gate. "I was up there checking the ceiling alarm when they broke through."

So that was where the Gee brothers had dug the well—and where the Political Officer and his gang planned to break in, thought Ming.

"I wish the general believed us," said Ming. "What did he mean when he said that you had disobeyed him again?"

"It is a long story." Shí sat on the floor against the wall. With his head hung low and his hands on his knees, he looked like a guilty child.

"Well, we have nothing else to do. Tell me!" Ming sat next to him, elbows balanced on his knees and chin resting on his bunched fists.

"If you insist."

The morning of my last battle as a human, my comrades and I gathered in front of General Wang. The sun rose above the distant plain, a red ball turning the earth and sky a deep shade of scarlet. He was standing on a wooden stage just inside the depot gates, flanked by the yellow flags of Qin. He wore a hat shaped like a hawk, which represented bravery and skill. His red silk cape fluttered in the wind, like a roaring flame licking at his burnished brass armor. I stared up at him in awe.

"The Mongol Khan is here to capture our depot's supplies!" His voice resonated like a brass bell. "You have all heard that every gust of wind is the dying breath of a laborer. With cold weather approaching, the Khan wants to kill two birds with one stone: feed his army and halt our Great Wall's construction."

He paused and surveyed us, a battalion of men in dark leather armor. "Will you let these barbarians steal from your loved ones working on the wall?"

"No!" we shouted, thrusting our spears and swords into the air.

"Then fight for your loved ones and for the grand rewards that await you! Today I will also grant the bravest among you the honor of accompanying the Emperor into his afterlife—by modeling for the terra-cotta army!"

Ming remembered the essay his bā ba had written about whether or not the terra-cotta soldiers were modeled after live soldiers. Bā ba had been right!

Feng and I looked at each other. I could tell what he was thinking before he spoke. "It is time to free my brother."

His brother, the village potter, had been crippled since birth. His pronounced limp had exempted him from serving in the army, but word had come that he had been drafted to work on the Emperor's mausoleum.

"So, you became a terra-cotta soldier because you were a hero?" Ming looked at his friend with admiration.

"Yes and no." Shí let out a deep sigh. "Even though modeling for the terra-cotta army was a new incentive, I had been ready to fight to free my father and to honor my family. But my heart sank when the general announced the battle formation—Reverse Flying Goose, shaped like an upside-down character for people, rén, 人."

As Ming pictured the deployment of the troops, he subconsciously traced a Y on the floor with his finger.

To mislead the enemy, the cavalry would hide at the rear and wait until our infantry—the shock troops—had engaged the Mongols on both flanks. We would take part in combat only if the enemy threatened to break through. General Wang had used this formation in the past. We knew that by the time we entered the battlefield, the enemy would have already been left headless or have retreated. General Wang was wary of ambushes, and so he forbade us from pursuing the enemy. The chances of us capturing a head were slim.

Ming sympathized with Shí's frustration. During the previous harvest, when the sparrows were eating the grain in the field, the village leaders had offered one yuán for every five sparrows killed. That was when Teacher Panda had taken the class to the Camel's Humps.

"I know you think you're smart," Teacher Panda had said to Ming mockingly. "So put away your slingshot and keep the tally for the class."

When his classmates had paraded through the village, displaying their trophies on long sticks, Ming, empty-handed and humiliated, had felt his face burn with frustration and embarrassment.

Our infantry marched out of the gates and past a line of drums as big as millstones sitting on wooden stands. I shifted with anticipation as the drummers hammered out a cadence with their thick mallets. My horse stirred beside me in response to the beating rhythm.

"Victory! Victory! Victory!" the shock troops shouted in unison, slamming their spear butts into the ground.

Feng and I glared at them in envy.

"Those guys are going to descend on the Mongols like a swarm of locusts and tear them apart!" Feng shouted over the sound of the drums.

"I just want to capture a few heads to free my father!" I shouted back.

"Why just free your father? Have some ambition! Don't

you want to be immortalized as a terra-cotta soldier?" Feng waved his sword in the air. "Just think about the glory you would bring to your family!"

"Not today," I replied. "The Mongols will be dead long before we join the fight."

"Relax. Their infantry is just bait." Feng gestured with his thumb. "General Wang is too smart to fall for that trick. You'll see." He paused as a mid-ranking officer rode toward us.

The officer pointed at us and called out, "You two!"

Feng and I bowed our heads. "Yes, sir!"

"Tell Captain Chu that General Wang has ordered him to hold half the infantry in reserve."

"Yes, Commander!" Feng shouted. We leaped onto our horses.

"What did I say?" he gloated. "Will I not make a great general one day? General Wang must suspect the Mongols are planning an ambush."

I swung into my saddle. "If you become a general, then I'll be the next Emperor of China," I shot back.

The drummers picked up the beat, signaling that the charge was about to begin. My heart pounded along with the speeding drums. Feng and I reached the shock troops.

Barely more than an arrow shot away, the enemy shuffled nervously in front of us.

We found Captain Chu at the head of the infantry formation. After we relayed the general's command to him, he ordered us to return to our unit.

I looked over at the eager shock troops. Something inside me suddenly snapped. My horse snorted, as if it opposed my decision. I had waited long enough. I would not miss this rare opportunity. I had to save my father, now.

Wheeling my horse around, I galloped straight at the enemy. My ears filled with the sound of rushing blood, and my vision was tinted a dark red.

Faintly I heard Captain Chu's enraged screams. The red curtain pulled back briefly when I remembered the harsh punishment that awaited disobedient soldiers. My fears vanished when I spotted Feng, riding alongside me, wearing a wild grin. Nothing mattered now. The bottle had broken and the soy sauce had spilled. I was going for the heads.

Laughing wildly, we unsheathed our swords and stampeded through the enemy infantry. We were like two foxes that had jumped into the chicken coop. The Mongols milled around us, eyes wide with surprise, squawking with confusion.

Ming tried to picture Shí hacking his way through a sea of startled, frightened Mongols.

Feng had been right about there being an ambush! Hundreds of Mongols emerged from hiding and charged onto the battlefield. I heard Captain Chu's battle cry as our shock troops slammed into the disarrayed Mongols like a landslide smashing a herd of wild cattle. As soon as our cavalry brothers joined the fray, the Mongols quickly scattered, dragging their wounded with them. By then, my saddle was heavy with enemy heads.

"Wow! Did you get a big reward?" asked Ming.

"Yes . . . but not exactly what I expected."

19
THE REWARD

THAT AFTERNOON, FENG AND I MARCHED SIDE BY side to the celebration banquet, proud and exhilarated. At last, I had fought like a hero. I held my head high, enjoying the feel of the moist autumn air on my face.

The sun faded from a brilliant yellow to a pale, washed-out pink. There was a festive atmosphere, with conversations bubbling all around us. A stage made of rough planks had been set up. In front of it, rows of long tables were piled high with large cuts of roasted meat, crispy scallion pancakes, and bowls of piping-hot noodles swimming in red chili sauce. The sharp fragrance rising from the overflowing jugs of sorghum wine heightened the savory aromas of the food.

I held my breath at the sight of two men dressed in black carrying a pair of wooden blocks. They placed them on the left side of the stage and then vanished into a nearby tent.

"How much land do you think I will be awarded?" Feng's question interrupted my thoughts. "You know I claimed six heads!" He smiled gleefully.

"A whole village, of course!" I said sarcastically. "I have only five, but that should be more than enough to free my father! Do you—"

My sentence was cut short when four men pushed a cart, creaking under the weight of wet clay, toward the stage. The black character Qín, 秦, was embroidered on their white workmen's robes, like a shield for their hearts.

Whispering broke out among the crowd.

"Sculptors for terra-cotta soldiers!"

"What an honor!"

"Not just for anyone," said Feng. "You have to be a hero!"

A grizzled soldier patted Feng on the shoulder and said,

"Maybe they'll model the *general* of the terra-cotta army after you."

"Then my spirit will be immortal and live forever!" Feng said with a smirk.

The murmuring stopped abruptly the moment General Wang stepped onto the stage.

"You all fought bravely today!" he declared. "We have destroyed the Mongol force and killed their Khan. Our depot is safe for now. I will reward the following accordingly.

"Shui Yang . . . one enemy head: two square miles of land.

"Wang Ting . . . two heads: four square miles of land.

"Xiao Ming . . . three heads: six square miles of land, and his family will be pardoned from mandatory labor.

"Wang Ren . . . four heads: eight square miles of land, and his family will . . ."

I played the abacus in my mind. With the five heads I had captured, I would be able to free my father *and* earn my family ten square miles of land—enough for us to live comfortably ever after.

Feng nudged me, a smug grin glued on his face like thick clay plaster. "Ready to be famous? We captured more heads than any of them." His grin widened.

"Yan Shí and Zhang Feng . . . report to the stage!"

Feng and I looked up. Captain Chu was walking toward us. His step was unhurried, but his face was grim. As he led us through the crowd, my neck grew slick with sweat, and a bubble of anxiety stirred in my stomach.

General Wang motioned us onto the stage. I glanced at Feng. His face was flushed with excitement. I struggled to draw in air.

General Wang addressed the crowd in a booming voice. "These are two of the most courageous and bravest Qin soldiers. I will free their families from manual labor and grant them each twenty square miles of land."

I was overwhelmed with joy. That was twice what I thought I would be awarded. I had done it! I was only fifteen years of age, and yet I had earned glory for my family! My father could return home, and my mother would never again go hungry!

The general continued. "Yet the Qin Army conquered China not solely because of its brave soldiers but also because of its strict rules and discipline." His words became cold and deliberate. "It takes self-restraint to be a true Qin warrior . . . These two must pay for their disobedience!"

My heart sank like an iron helmet in a lake. Whispering broke out like a roiling pot of hot congee. Four large men dressed in black emerged from the tent. The lower parts of their faces were covered with red scarves, and large axes were strapped to their belts.

Silently, they walked onto the stage. They grabbed our arms and twisted them behind us. The men dragged us to the blocks. I looked at Feng. His features had frozen in a look of shock. Beads of perspiration stood out on his forehead.

"But that's not fair! You were heroes!" Anger and outrage stirred inside Ming.

Shí ignored Ming's interruption and continued.

Feng fell to his knees beside me. His eyes seemed to roam with no particular sense of purpose. In an unsteady voice he said, "I am prepared to pay for my actions."

"I am too." I dropped to my knees, a turmoil of confusion, terror, despair, and resignation surging through me.

"I will grant you both a quick death and the honor of guarding the Emperor in his afterlife." The general's voice softened. "These men"—he pointed at the sculptors standing next to the wagon piled with clay—"will give you a new life following your execution."

"Do you have a last request?" asked one of the executioners in a deep voice.

"Yes!" said Feng. He had regained his composure and now addressed the sculptors, who were standing beside the stage. "Brothers! Make sure you do justice to my handsome face!"

But nobody laughed at his joke.

"I have one," I said, lifting my head and trying to hide my sorrow. "I wish to face south, toward my village, so my spirit can find its way home."

The grip on my arms loosened. The executioner looked at General Wang, who nodded gravely. The men moved the blocks and turned us to face south, looking over the crowd. In the distance, the sky was overcast, as deep and dark as a freshly dug grave.

"I will see you in the afterlife, Feng!" I whispered.

"You'd better. I don't want to spend eternity with strangers." He tried to sound lighthearted, but his voice faltered.

Looking down, I saw our cavalry brothers stand and raise their hands in a salute. Other squads followed suit. I laid my head on the block.

My heart was filled with a pain and sadness that I had not known could exist in life. I would never have a chance to care for my aging parents and fulfill my obligation as a dutiful son. But my despair was tempered by the knowledge that, because of what I had done, they would have a better life.

A gust of wind surged across the plain. The distant storm was racing toward us. I detected a hint of evergreen and the raw, earthy scent of clay. The thunder rolled closer. Through my tears I saw my mother standing at our door, her arms held out to me.

The ax whistled through the air, and then . . . nothing.

Grass plains of China.

20
TOMB ROBBERS

MING WAS ABOUT TO ASK SHÍ WHAT IT WAS LIKE TO "wake up" as a terra-cotta soldier, when the sound of drums stopped him.

Ming stood and peered through the window into the corridor. "What's that?"

Shí remained seated. "Just the signal to change shifts."

Two soldiers walked through the moon gate. They stopped in front of one of the lions. One tugged its tail. A secret door that blended in with the fishing net on the wall slid open. The soldiers disappeared through it.

A dissonant clanging of gongs and clackers suddenly drowned out the drumming. Shí sprang to his feet.

"And *that*?" Ming asked.

"That's the alarm!" said Shí.

A group of soldiers burst out of the secret door, swords in hand. Feng and Si Ji were among them. Just as the door closed, there was an earth-shattering explosion. Two shelves in the storage room toppled over, scattering papers and broken porcelain all around. Through the window, Shí and Ming saw the ceiling in front of the moon gate cave in. Falling debris crushed several of the soldiers. A cloud of smoke engulfed the corridor.

Broken terra-cotta soldiers in the tomb of Emperor Qin.

"They've broken in, Ming!" Shí pressed his face against the lattice. "You were right about the sticks!"

The dust settled slowly. Ming and Shí watched as Feng and Si Ji backed away from the gaping hole in the ceiling. A rope ladder snaked down. The terra-cotta soldiers stood still against the wall as men in Mao-style uniforms climbed down the rope, one after another. Each had a rifle strapped to his back. Their dark silhouettes flickered on the wall like shadow puppets. Ming counted ten men in all.

Shí pointed to the tall bald man leading the group and whispered, "He was at the Political Officer's house!"

The leader looked up at the purple lanterns and slipped his flashlight and a two-way radio into his belt. He gestured for his men to follow. One of the men knocked his fist on Feng's chest. Ming couldn't hear what he was saying, but the others seemed to be amused by the hollow sound. Their nervous laughter swirled through the corridor.

"Why don't the soldiers attack them?" asked Ming.

"Patience," said Shí, eyes fixed on the intruders as they walked along the corridor toward them.

The robbers stopped to marvel at the treasures around

them. They examined the ivory fishermen and traced their fingers over the silver fishing nets. One even tried to pry a golden fish off the wall with his knife, grunting in frustration when the steel tip snapped off.

Ming noticed Feng subtly press his hand against one of the fish. Above the intruders, the pearl stars in the ceiling opened. It took the distracted robbers a moment to notice the fine cloud of yellow powder drifting down.

Shí patted Ming on the back. "Well done on fixing the trap!"

The robbers started coughing violently and shielded their eyes. Some cried out in panic.

Ming's body tensed as he watched more of the powder float down. He thought he tasted something intensely bitter, almost like tar. Panicking, he gasped, his face flushing beet red.

Shí quickly took hold of one of Ming's hands and dug his finger into the web between the thumb and the index finger. A tingling sensation traveled through Ming's hand. "Keep breathing!" Shí instructed. "The poison is too far away to harm you. The Valley of Harmony acupressure point should calm you."

Gradually, Ming felt he could breathe easily again.

When he looked back into the corridor, he was shocked by what he saw. Some robbers lay motionless on the ground. Others were trying to scramble through the rubble toward the section of corridor with the cherry blossoms, away from the yellow dust. A few fired their rifles wildly. Several terra-cotta soldiers were struck and broke into pieces. One bullet punched through the storage room's thick wooden door, shattering one of the porcelain stools. Ming ducked down.

"No, you will want to watch this." Shí pulled Ming up to the window.

The leader of the robbers, now blinded by the poison dust, tried to navigate by tapping his hand against the wall. When his fingers touched one of the cherry blossoms, thin needles shot out from the center of each of the flowers. Twitching and screaming, the men yanked the needles out of their bodies and ran into one another, as if they were possessed by demons. Then they collapsed.

Ming leaned against the wall, breathing deeply and hugging himself. He couldn't stop shaking.

"Are you all right?" Shí asked anxiously.

Ming wiped his face with sweaty fingers. "Are they dead?"

"No. The snake venom on the needles will only temporarily paralyze them."

The door to the corridor swung open. Shí quickly turned, fists raised, ready to face the intruder.

21
THE WALKIE-TALKIE

GENERAL WANG WALKED IN.

"Was the explosion caused by the dynamite you warned us about?"

Shí stood at attention. "Yes, sir. They have a large box of it."

"What about the weapons that shattered my soldiers?"

"They're called guns," Ming said.

Turning to Ming, the general said, "Some of my men are in pieces out there because I did not listen to you. The explosion damaged the moon gate and almost set off the tomb's self-destruction system." He pointed a finger upward. "I am sure there are more robbers up there. I can defeat enemies armed with swords or spears, but I can't fight against opponents with these powerful new weapons. If they try again, I am afraid they will trip the self-destruct mechanism, destroying my army and the entire tomb, including the Emperor. Can you help us?"

"Yes, sir!" said Shí eagerly.

"Not you. I mean your friend. Ming, can you advise me?"

Ming forced himself to look up at the general. He racked his mind for ideas, but anxiety and uncertainty made him dizzy. His head was as empty as a bowl licked by a hungry dog.

A crackling sound drew their attention to the corridor, where Feng and Si Ji were reassembling a broken terra-cotta soldier. The sound came from the two-way radio.

"What's that?" asked General Wang.

"It's called a walkie-talkie. You use it to talk to people who are far away," Ming explained. An idea sparked. "Maybe we can use it to lure the remaining robbers into a trap!"

"Can you do that?" the general asked thoughtfully. "If

we can get them down here, we can handle them." He grimaced. "Unfortunately, the explosion cut us off from the main tomb, where most of my soldiers are stationed. So we must respond to this situation ourselves."

Ming could not help glancing toward the robbers lying in the corridor. Although he knew that they had planned to harm his bā ba, he didn't relish the idea of killing them or any of the others. "What are you going to do to them?" he asked softly.

The general seemed to read Ming's mind. "Remember," he said, "these men are pitiless. They would not hesitate to hurt you or anyone standing in their way. There is no place for mercy on the battlefield."

Ming knew the general was right. The robbers expected to have his bā ba take the blame and wouldn't think twice about damaging or even destroying the tomb.

"Please, Ming, we need your help," said Shí.

"Yes . . . I can try," Ming agreed.

The group moved into the corridor. Ming's legs shook as he carefully picked his way between the bodies of the unconscious robbers. He saw yellow saliva dripping from the corner of the leader's mouth. His eyes were milky white, reminding Ming of a dead fish. As Ming bent over, he smelled the man's foul breath. Repressing the urge to retch, he quickly wrested the walkie-talkie from the leader's grasp.

There was thick static, and then a blurry, metallic-sounding voice. "What's ha—? . . . *Pschshh.*"

Ming studied the radio in his hand. General Wang, Shí, Feng, Si Ji, and the other soldiers watched him intently. He removed the back from the walkie-talkie and found a loose wire. He carefully reattached the wire, snapped the cover back on, and adjusted the dial. The static disappeared, and a man's voice poured out.

"Report! Report! Why was there shooting?"

Ming muted the volume. He looked at General Wang for instructions.

"Shí, go with Ming. Lead the robbers down the pit corridor. Feng, Si Ji—you are in charge of cleaning up here."

Ming turned the sound back on.

"Answer me!" The voice from the radio sounded louder and angry. "What's going on down there?"

Ming held the walkie-talkie to his mouth and pushed the button down, making a faint *click*. In his deepest voice he said, "Everything is under control. A coward was frightened by shadows." He released the button. *Clack.*

"But did you find anything?"

Click. "Yes! We found a gold statue. It's enormous. We need everyone's help, but first we need to scout for traps. Wait for my instructions." *Clack.*

"Hurry—we don't have much time before sunrise."

General Wang pointed at the wall. Shí tugged the lion's tail, and the secret door slid open. Ming followed him through it into a corridor illuminated by the sooty, dim glow of blue lanterns. He was captivated by a vivid mural of a massive battle, with soldiers locked in eternal combat.

An early-fourteenth-century watercolor of mounted warriors pursuing enemies, believed to be Mongols.

Shí stopped abruptly. "Ming, once the robbers come into the pit corridor, you must lead them far enough in so that you reach this horse." He pointed to a large white horse on the wall, standing on its rear legs, head up, as if it were ready to jump out of the scene. "A trap door will open, and they will drop into a prison cell."

"It's bright here." Ming knitted his brow. "They'll see me."

"I can take care of that!" Shí pressed his hand to the mural, touching a flaming rock that was hurtling from a catapult through the air. Instantly, the lanterns were extinguished, leaving them in darkness.

Ming pulled out his flashlight and turned it on. He brought the walkie-talkie to his mouth again. *Click.* "Come down! Follow my flashlight." *Clack.*

The walkie-talkie crackled. "OK, we're coming!"

Ming crept closer to the opening, holding the flashlight steady.

A group of men entered the passageway. Ming slowly backed up toward Shí.

The men cautiously moved forward.

"Deng?" a chubby man at the front, caught in the flashlight's glow, called out. "Is that you?"

Ming's heartbeat quickened. He could sense that Shí was near him. Without replying, he waved the light up and down, luring the men farther along the corridor. The moment Ming passed the white horse, Shí pressed on the horse's tail.

The lanterns flared to life, and the floor before them opened. A wave of ear-piercing screams filled the space, and the robbers disappeared from view.

The floor shut, leaving Ming and Shí alone. An ominous silence filled the corridor.

22

SACRIFICE THE ARM, SAVE THE BODY

GENERAL WANG LED A SQUAD OF SOLDIERS INTO THE pit corridor. He smiled down at Ming. "Good job! You would have made an exemplary Qin soldier."

Ming bowed his head and tried to suppress his grin.

Turning to Shí, General Wang said, "The Emperor is safe again, thanks to both of you!"

Ming shook his head and said, "Sir, their leader, the Political Officer, is not among them. He will come with reinforcements. And so will others."

General Wang frowned. "We have all sworn to protect

the Emperor for eternity. We will fight to the end. But I fear that another explosion will cause the tomb to self-destruct."

He turned and headed into the fishermen corridor, with Ming and Shí trailing behind him. There they found Feng, Si Ji, and other soldiers loading the paralyzed robbers onto stretchers.

A thought struck Ming. "I wonder . . ."

General Wang stopped and looked at him with a newfound respect. "What are you thinking, Ming?"

"If I can prove to the museum that this is Emperor Qin's tomb, they will take special care to protect it, treating everything inside with the utmost respect."

From General Wang's puzzled expression, Ming realized that he should define "museum."

"A museum is where the government displays old and important objects for people to study and see. They are responsible for excavating and caring for artifacts."

"How can you be so certain they will protect us?" asked the general.

"Our leader, Chairman Mao, greatly admires Emperor Qin. I don't think he'll allow anyone to destroy his tomb.

One thing I'm certain of is that now that robbers know where you are, more of them will come. The Emperor's tomb is no longer safe."

"In that case, we must sacrifice the arm to save the body!" General Wang made a fist. "We will seal the Emperor's chambers and reveal ourselves to protect him. If anyone ever breaks into the Emperor's chambers, the final trap will destroy the tomb. I hope it never comes to that."

General Wang reached into a leather satchel on his hip and fished out a yellow silk pouch. "Take this! It's the Emperor's chop—his official seal. Show it to your museum officials."

A royal chop, or stamp, was used instead of a signature on documents and orders.

Ming accepted the heavy pouch. His hands were shaking with excitement and anxiety. He realized that with the

Political Officer still up there, Bā ba and the tomb would never be safe. If he failed to convince the museum directors, he would lose everything dear to him. He unbuttoned his cotton jacket and carefully put the pouch in his inner pocket.

"Shí, you go with Ming. Help and protect your friend," ordered General Wang. "Let me accompany you to the frog exit."

He turned abruptly and led the way back toward the armory. Ming and Shí followed in single file. Ming waved as they passed Feng and Si Ji. The two were now placing broken terra-cotta soldiers into large woven bamboo baskets.

Suddenly, a gunshot broke the silence.

Ming dove to the ground. General Wang pulled out his sword with lightning speed.

Ming looked back and saw Feng and Si Ji run over to Shí, who was lying on top of one of the tomb robbers. Ming rushed to them.

"What happened?" General Wang demanded.

Feng's and Si Ji's eyes were wide with panic. In a broken voice, Feng said, "A robber regained consciousness.

He fired his gun at Ming. Shí flung himself on the thief to protect Ming."

"He crushed the enemy with his body," Si Ji added mournfully, kneeling beside Shí.

"But he'll be OK—right?" Ming asked desperately. "I mean, he was in pieces when I first saw him!"

Shí was lying facedown on the ground. There was a large hole in the back of his head where Old Tian's signature seal had once been.

Feng's face was drawn with grief. "No, Ming. His seal is gone. Without it, he's . . . he's lifeless."

Ming desperately ran his hands through the rubble around Shí. "Yes, yes, I know. But we'll find it! We *have* to find it!" The thought of losing Shí drove him to tears. Si Ji brought down a lantern from the ceiling. Feng and the other terra-cotta soldiers dropped to their hands and knees, rummaging around Shí.

General Wang grabbed Ming's arm. "We do not have time, Ming! You need to complete your mission."

Ming stood up, fighting to control his sobbing. He knew that Shí would want him to be strong. Now he was even more determined to save his new friends and the tomb. He would take the back road out of the village. He would run, walk, or crawl to Xi'an. He just hoped he wouldn't be too late to save these terra-cotta soldiers, the tomb . . . and his bā ba.

"Yes, sir! I'll be back!" Ming dashed away.

23
THE TRAP

THE GARDEN WAS BRIGHTLY ILLUMINATED. MING wondered whether the lanterns had been lit the whole time or had somehow sensed his approach and re-ignited. When he reached the pond, he bent over, separated waxy green leaves, and found the frog frozen in midleap. As soon as he twisted the head off its body, the door began to grind open.

With the frog's head in hand, Ming ran down the short tunnel and out the door. Soft dawn light was peeking through the ceiling, illuminating the entrance cave. Ming quickly placed the head back on the body of the headless frog.

Resting briefly on his heels and catching his breath, he watched the door close behind him.

"Ming!"

Startled, Ming turned. He could hardly believe his eyes. "Bā ba!" he cried.

At that moment, someone kicked him, sending him sprawling on the ground. The detonation of pain inside his stomach was unlike any he'd experienced.

The Political Officer loomed above him. "Ha! So this is where you're hiding your treasure! Where is my terracotta statue?"

Goat Face straddled Ming and pinned his arms to the ground. Ming struggled to break free.

"Don't hurt him!" Old Chen shouted. Although his hands were tied behind his back, he charged into the Political Officer with his shoulder and knocked him off Ming.

Ming gasped for air and struggled to stand. The Political Officer sprang to his feet and swung at Ming, landing a punch below his rib cage. A burst of pain shot through

Ming's body. He collapsed and curled up into a ball, struggling for breath. His eyes watered.

"Stop!" Bā ba stumbled up and pushed himself between Ming and the Political Officer.

Goat Face shoved Bā ba away. He grabbed hold of Ming's hair and pointed his pistol at his temple. "You think you're smarter than me. But you forgot about your footprints in the snow! Now, show me how to get inside or I'll kill you both!" He fired a shot at the cave floor. It echoed like a firecracker.

Ears buzzing, Ming sucked in a partial breath. He rallied his thoughts and gestured at the dragon.

"What's that?" The Political Officer's eyes locked on the jade ball. He shoved Ming aside. "I don't need you. I know how to open this door."

He stood in front of the dragon. Eyes alight with greed, he reached for the jade ball.

Two metal darts shot out of the dragon's eyes. Goat Face had no time to react. Like a sack of flour, he fell to the ground with a thud.

Ming turned and saw his bā ba staring in terrified wonder at Goat Face's body. "Are you all right?" Ming asked. He quickly untied the ropes binding his bā ba. Old Chen's face was haggard and his eyes red, but joy shone through his smile.

Bā ba hugged Ming tightly. "The colonel did an excellent job in the general's absence."

Dragon face carved on stone.

24
VISITORS

THE SUN HAD BROKEN AWAY FROM THE HORIZON. Dazzling yellow beams streamed through the gaps in the dense pine trees. Scattered pools of light splashed on Ming and his bā ba as they walked back home. Although he was exhausted, Ming described in detail all that had happened—assembling Shí . . . eating worms . . . entering the tomb . . . meeting General Wang . . . experiencing the dynamite explosion . . . seeing the tomb robbers foiled by the traps.

Bā ba didn't know what to make of Ming's account of

his adventures. After a long silence, Old Chen wrapped his arm around Ming's shoulder, pulling him close in a tender way. "That's a great story, son! You've outdone the old men at the teahouse! Now tell me what really happened."

Ming was reaching for the seal when he spotted a jeep parked in front of their house. His heart skipped a beat, and he turned to Bā ba with a look of concern. Had they come to arrest him? Should they run?

An old man with gray hair and thin eyes got out of the backseat. "Ah, Chen, I have been waiting for you! I am sorry I missed you when you came to Xi'an yesterday. I was in Beijing."

It was Director Gu of the Xi'an museum, Bā ba's friend. Ming let out his breath.

Director Gu took hold of Bā ba's hand. "We have to close your office. I know this is hard for you, so I came to inform you personally. I tried to change the board's decision, but I failed."

Ming looked at the two adults. He knew this was the moment. He pulled the silk pouch out of his pocket and offered it to the director. "I think this will change your mind," he said with confidence.

For a moment, both men looked puzzled. Then the director accepted the pouch from Ming.

Slowly and carefully he took out the heavy gold seal. He held it in his hand, then turned it over and studied it. Suddenly, he froze and stared at it in disbelief. The silence seemed to stretch for an eternity. Finally, he blurted, "My goodness, it's—"

"Yes, it's from Emperor Qin's tomb!" Ming's face lit up with a grin. "My bā ba found it!"

Bā ba stared at Ming with wide eyes.

25
THREE MONTHS LATER

SUMMER CAME EARLY. SHORT SLEEVES REPLACED spring jackets. As the sun rose over Li Mountain, it shone like a burning rice cake, scorching the excavation site. The air was thick with the fragrance of growing wheat, grass, and wildflowers from the surrounding fields. Around the archaeological site was a sea of blooming color—green, yellow, purple, and white—as if the earth were bursting into song.

It seemed that all three hundred Red Star villagers had gathered at the site, along with many visitors. Ming recognized kids and adults from neighboring villages. They were sitting, squatting, or standing on the packed dirt around a temporary wooden stage. Some wore broad straw hats to block the burning sun, while others held their hands over their eyes or squinted against the harsh light. Despite the perspiration glinting on their foreheads, they talked and bustled with the energy of a village market before New Year.

Teacher Panda led her awestruck and excited students through the crowd. Ming and his classmates gathered around her in the shade of a large cottonwood tree.

"Ming, I have a new slingshot. Would you like me to show you after school?" asked a boy.

"No, he can't," replied the boy with glasses. "Ming is going to show me his new radio."

"Ming, you're so smart!" The red-cheeked girl smiled eagerly at him.

"And so brave!" a pretty girl with two ponytails chipped in.

Ming looked uneasily at Teacher Panda, remembering how she had often yelled at him for talking to his classmates. Instead, she smiled benevolently at them.

On the stage, a group of young men were following

the rhythm of the èr hú player, clapping cymbals and banging drums. The singer stood in the middle of the stage, pantomiming climbing a mountain, riding a horse, and swimming in a river. He raised both his hands and one of his legs as he finished his song.

We would climb a thousand mountains
And cross a thousand rivers
To follow our dear Chairman Mao.

The three Gee brothers lit a long string of firecrackers, biān pào, 鞭炮, sending fountains of sparks rising into the air and bits of burned paper fluttering down on the cheering crowd. Never before had Red Star seen a celebration like this!

When the Regional Secretary, a young woman, moved onto the stage, the musicians quickly retreated. She was accompanied by a stout, stocky man. The noise died down, and all eyes focused on them.

"Allow me to introduce Red Star's new Political Officer, Comrade Ding!" the woman said in a high, sweet voice. "He will guide us in adhering to dear Chairman Mao's teachings."

Comrade Ding was dressed in a new Mao-style uniform. He raised his hand and waited until the clapping had quieted down. "Dear villagers of Red Star! Today we are here to celebrate the ground breaking of the Terra-Cotta Museum. The central government in Beijing plans to turn Red Star into a city to rival the metropolis of Xi'an! Not only are we going to have a forest of high-rise apartment buildings—complete with indoor bathrooms!—but we will also have two large movie theaters and a boulevard broad enough for four large trucks to drive abreast, lined with modern shops and hotels. When that day comes, darkness will never fall over Red Star. At night, neon signs and lights hanging like melons from lampposts will light the city as bright as day. Your lives will be as sweet as a jar of honey."

His speech was like a drop of water in a pot of hot oil; the crowd bubbled and sizzled with excitement.

The new Political Officer waited a moment before resuming his speech. "Now, let me introduce you to the director of the new Terra-Cotta Museum. He and his brave son single-handedly lifted the veil of mystery from Emperor Qin's tomb and captured the tomb robbers!"

Whispers broke out in the crowd.

"I heard those robbers all went insane in the city jail," said an old woman.

"I heard they each tried to outdo the other in telling crazy stories about living terra-cotta soldiers, fishermen who shoot poison, and magic lanterns!" Teacher Panda piped up.

"It must be the mercury in the tomb that drove them mad," said a toothless old man.

Ming's bā ba stood up from beneath a gingko tree. The villagers chattered and clapped excitedly. All eyes followed the Regional Secretary as she hurried off the stage with a red cloth that had been folded and twisted into the shape of a flower. She pinned the flower on Ming's bā ba's chest.

The villagers' cheers echoed the squawks of the happy geese in the sky.

"I have an announcement too," Teacher Panda said in a voice loud enough for the Political Officer to hear. He waved her onto the stage.

Teacher Panda looked at Ming, her lips curled back like dry bean pods into a smile. "I am pleased to declare Ming a model Young Pioneer, so that other children can follow his example of bravery and dedication to the Revolution! He is the pride of our school and Red Star!"

Everyone clapped and cheered.

Ming was caught off guard, and a blush rose to his cheeks. He suddenly thought of his mother and fought to hold back his tears. How proud and happy she would have been.

"With that," declared Comrade Ding, "let the celebration continue!"

"Ming, please show us where the tomb robbers broke in!" The ponytail girl's plea interrupted Ming's bittersweet thoughts.

"Who else wants to see?" Ming asked.

"Me! Me! Me!" His classmates pushed one another to get closer to him.

Ming led the way along the narrow ridge that divided large pits filled with rows of excavated soldiers, some still half buried, others missing heads, arms, or legs. Archaeologists scurried around in the trenches like ants.

He stopped in front of a column of soldiers led by General Wang. His classmates gaped in awe at the statues and their armor.

"Ahead is where the secret traps captured the robbers." Ming pointed.

"I want to see it!" several of his classmates exclaimed. They rushed passed Ming. General Wang winked at him. Ming bowed his head and exchanged smiles with Feng and Si Ji.

Ming's eyes were suddenly drawn to a nearby archaeologist. The man was squatting in a pit, holding a small clay square up to the sunlight, examining it with a magnifying glass. Ming saw the familiar character and raced down into the pit. He apologized and swiftly snatched the square out of the man's hands. Ignoring the cries of the archaeologist and his startled classmates, he dashed back up the steep path and into a large tent next to the pit.

Soldiers with missing arms or heads were lined up. In one corner of the tent, a soldier stood with his back to the entrance, whole except for a gap at the nape of his neck. Ming ran over and carefully fit the chip into the opening.

A bright light blinded him.

"What took you so long, Ming?" Shí's voice boomed.

Terra-cotta soldiers and horses in the tomb of Emperor Qin.

GLOSSARY

1	**father**	bā ba	爸爸
9	**field**	tián	田
12	**"Serve the People"**	wèi rén mín fú wù	为人民服务
19	**stone**	Shí	石
22	**China**	Zhōng Gúo	中国
22	***History of Qin***	Qín Shi	秦史
24	**Great Wall**	Cháng Chéng	长城
37	**teahouse**	Chá Guǎn	茶馆
38	**unit of money**	yuán	元
99	**dumplings**	jiǎo zi	饺子
100	**vital energy**	yuán qì	元气
120	**awl**	zhuī zi	锥子

128	dragon	lóng	龙
128	phoenix	fèng	凤
135	wood	mù	木
135	fire	huǒ	火
135	earth	tǔ	土
135	metal	jīn	金
135	water	shuǐ	水
136	emperor	huáng	皇
137	bravery	dǎn	胆
137	discipline	lǜ	律
137	loyalty	zhōng	忠
137	glory	róng	荣
138	name of a dynasty	Qín	秦
153	"double happiness"	xǐ	囍
198	firecracker	biān pào	鞭炮
209	a surname meaning "ocean" or "victory"	Yíng	瀛

Authors Ying and Vinson Compestine with one of the three farmers who discovered the first terra-cotta soldier. Vinson is holding the hoe that struck the terra-cotta head.

The authors pose with contemporary replicas of the sculptures meant for tourists.

AUTHORS' NOTE

FOR YEARS, WE TALKED ABOUT WRITING A BOOK together, but we couldn't find a project that interested both of us—that is, until we visited Qin Shi Huang's mausoleum.

In Xian, we were introduced to one of the three farmers who unearthed the first terra-cotta soldier. He invited us to his home, where we interviewed him and listened to his account of the discovery in 1974. Afterwards, we visited the Xian Terra-cotta Museum and witnessed how craftsmen use ancient methods in their workshop to mass-produce terra-cotta replicas for tourists. Later on, as we explored the surrounding countryside and the unearthed portions of Emperor Qin's tomb in Li Mountain, we heard more fascinating stories.

Upon returning to the United States, we read every

book we could find about Emperor Qin and his terra-cotta army. The historical facts intensified our interest and stirred our imaginations. What secrets were still locked away in the Emperor's tomb—and what would it be like to "stand guard" for thousands of years?

Vinson was captivated by the stories of ancient battles, the paraphernalia of warfare, the rumors of secret traps in the tomb, and, particularly, the terra-cotta soldiers. As we plotted out the story, he developed a strong affinity for the characters Ming and Shí—who in the book are only slightly younger than he was at that time.

Ying, nine years old, dressed in Mao's uniform, in Wuhan, China. 1972.

Ever since Ying was young, she has been fascinated by Emperor Qin because they share an uncommon bond. In China, all names have meanings. For example, Tian, 田, the name of the sculptor who created Shí, means "field." Before the emperor titled himself Qin Shi Huang—literally, "first Emperor Qin"—his surname was also 瀛 Ying. It is one of the most difficult written Chinese words, a combination of six different characters: *water, perish, mouth, month, female,* and *ordinary*; together, the characters can mean either "ocean" or "victory." In this book, Ying wanted to portray what life was like during Mao's regime. When the first terra-cotta soldiers were discovered, toward the end of the Cultural Revolution (1966–76), she was about the same age as Ming. Like him, she was singled out at school by her classmates and criticized by her teacher for being from an intellectual family, and had to endure endless political study.

Our combined interests led us to write this historical novel based on true events that took place under two ruthless dictators from modern and ancient times: Mao Zedong and Ying Zheng.

Mao Zedong ruled China from 1949 to 1976. In 1958,

Mao Zedong. The slogan on top reads, "All anti-revolutionaries are paper tigers."

he launched the Great Leap Forward, an ill-conceived campaign to modernize China. It resulted in a famine that claimed millions of lives. The modernization campaign's failure severely weakened Mao's grip on power. In 1966, he started a movement called the Cultural Revolution, in a bid to eliminate his political rivals and regain absolute control over China. His followers elevated him to an object of worship. Each day, citizens had to sing revolutionary songs and read Mao's teachings. Class time was reserved for studying Communist revolutionary history and political dogma. Pins with Mao's portrait were popular accessories, and it was fashionable to wear Mao-style uniforms and hats.

Mao banned—and burned—many books. Those who opposed his policies, namely teachers and intellectuals, were killed or exiled to labor camps or remote villages. Mao often compared himself to Emperor Qin, emulating Qin Shi Huang's aggressive use of censorship and indoctrination to maintain his power. In one of his speeches, Mao stated that he had far outdone Qin Shi Huang in his attack on intellectuals: "He buried 460 scholars alive; we have buried 46,000 scholars alive. . . . You [intellectuals] revile us for being Qin Shi Huangs. You are wrong. We have surpassed Qin Shi Huang a hundredfold."

Ying Zheng became king of Qin at the age of thirteen. Qin was one of seven kingdoms during the Warring States period (from about 475 to 221 BCE). By the time he was twenty-five, King Qin had defeated the other six states, unifying China. He divided the new country into thirty-six prefectures and proclaimed himself Qin Shi Huang, the First Emperor of Qin.

During the Warring States period, Sun Tzu, a prominent general from the state of Wu, wrote *The Art of War*, a book about military strategy and discipline. The book's tactics guided many rulers of ancient China, and still influences military and political leaders today.

The Qin army was famous for its brilliant strategies and strict discipline. It was also renowned for its courageous soldiers and generous incentive system. It's hard to believe, but it actually was standard practice for Emperors and generals in ancient China to reward brave soldiers who brought them enemy heads.

Emperor Qin is a controversial historical figure. He standardized the systems of weights, measurements, and currency, as well as the Chinese written language; he built roads and canals to facilitate trade throughout the empire; and he constructed the Great Wall to secure the northern border against pillaging Mongols—nomadic tribes led by rulers called khans. However, during the construction of the Great Wall, strict quotas and harsh working conditions resulted in hundreds of thousands of deaths. To strengthen his regime, Emperor Qin buried alive Confucian scholars, or "intellectuals," and burned writings that he believed threatened or challenged his imperial power.

Obsessed with immortality, Emperor Qin took mercury potions, which his physicians believed would extend his life. On the contrary, he suffered the painful effects of mercury poisoning, becoming irrational and paranoid.

To prepare for his eternal life, he commanded that a massive, elaborate mausoleum be built beneath a burial mound 377 feet (115 meters) in height and measuring 1,132 feet (345 meters) from east to west, and 1,148 feet (350 meters) from north to south. The mound later became known as Li Mountain. There are one hundred pits and tombs surrounding the burial chamber, and the construction took thirty-nine years, from 247 to 208 BCE.

Emperor Qin died at the age of forty-nine. In 206 BCE, four years after his death, his dynasty was overthrown by General Xi'ang Yu, whose army destroyed all of the aboveground structures and looted part of the outer mound of the underground palace. According to historian Sima Qian's record from the Han dynasty, written about a hundred years after Qin's death, Xi'ang Yu's army stole treasure and weapons from the terra-cotta soldiers and set a fire that burned for three months.

Sima Qian wrote, "The tomb was filled with models of palaces, pavilions, and offices as well as fine vessels, precious stones, and rarities." Deadly traps like hidden crossbows, poisonous powders, and a massive terra-cotta army of life-size soldiers armed with real bronze weapons, guarded the tomb.

In 1974, while digging a well near Xi Yang Village, east of Xi'an, three farmers unearthed a terra-cotta soldier. Since then, over eight thousand terra-cotta soldiers and many other artifacts have been uncovered. Because each soldier's face is unique, many historians believe that actual soldiers modeled for the statues.

To this day, the emperor's main tomb is still shrouded in mystery and remains unexcavated. Geological surveys have found high levels of mercury where the main chamber is believed to be located. For years, archaeologists have debated as to why, unlike other ancient tombs in China, Emperor Qin's mausoleum hasn't suffered further plundering. Perhaps it's because the intruders fear the mercury, the Emperor's curses, or the rumored traps and self-destruct mechanism. Or perhaps the burial mound was simply too thick for anyone to break through until modern times, after farmers had cut down the trees on Li Mountain, resulting in massive soil loss from erosion.

According to the Chinese government, there is no plan to open the main burial chamber for fear of mercury leaking into the surrounding area or triggering a trap that would cause the entire mausoleum to self-destruct. There are additional apprehensions about preserving the contents of the tomb once opened. "It is best to keep the ancient tomb untouched, because of the complex conditions inside," Duan Qinbao, a researcher with the Shaanxi Provincial Archaeology Institute, said in 2006.

We hope this book will pique your interest in China and fuel your fascination about the secrets of Emperor Qin's mausoleum!

MING'S FAVORITE STIR-FRIED NOODLES, WITH WORMS

If you have difficulty obtaining Giant Carnivorous Li Mountain Worms, substitute chicken, beef, or tofu for protein. We do not advise using the variety of worms found in most household backyards or parks, as they do not taste very good.

When cooking for good friends and on special occasions, top the noodles with crispy pan-fried eggs, as Shí did for Ming.

YIELD: 4 SERVINGS

- 8 ounces Giant Carnivorous Li Mountain Worms, or precut stir-fry chicken or beef, or thin-sliced tofu
- 2 tablespoons store-bought chili-garlic sauce or soy sauce
- 2 teaspoons cornstarch

- 8 ounces silver needle noodles or spaghetti
- 2 tablespoons olive or canola oil
- 1/2 tablespoon minced garlic
- 1/2 tablespoon minced fresh ginger
- 1 1/2 cups chopped daikon or 1 package shredded carrots
- 2 tablespoons soy sauce
- 2 teaspoons toasted sesame oil
- Salt and pepper to taste

PAN-FRIED EGGS

- 2 tablespoons olive or canola oil
- 2 teaspoons black or white sesame seeds
- 4 large eggs
- 1/8 teaspoon salt
- 1/4 teaspoon ground black pepper
- 2 tablespoons soy sauce

Combine the worms or meat with the chili-garlic sauce and cornstarch. Toss to coat. Cover and refrigerate for 15 minutes or longer. While the worms marinate, cook the noodles according to package directions. Drain and rinse with cold water to prevent sticking. Set aside.

Heat the oil in a large skillet over medium-high heat.

Add the garlic and ginger. Stir-fry until the garlic is lightly browned, about 2 minutes. Add the worms. Stir-fry until the worms are no longer pink, about 2 minutes. Add the daikon and stir-fry for 1 minute. Add the noodles and soy sauce. Cook and stir until the noodles are heated through, about 1 minute. Stir in the sesame oil and season with salt and pepper.

FOR THE EGGS

Heat the oil in a medium nonstick skillet over medium heat and swirl to coat. Sprinkle in the sesame seeds and toast until fragrant, about a minute. Crack 2 of the eggs into one side of the pan; crack the remaining 2 eggs into the other side. Swirl the pan gently, letting the egg whites flow together, forming one large piece.

Sprinkle the salt and pepper over the eggs. Cook until the egg whites are crispy and brown on the bottom and the yolks are firmly set, about 3 minutes. Keeping them in one piece, flip the eggs using a wide spatula and cook until the whites turn crispy and brown on the other side, about 1 to 2 minutes.

Pour the soy sauce over the eggs. Simmer for 30 seconds, turning the eggs once to coat the other side. Serve over the noodles and drizzle with the pan sauce.

ACKNOWLEDGMENTS

First and foremost, we'd like to thank our editor, Howard Reeves, for seeing the potential in our story while it was still a sprout and for his tireless efforts to nurture it into a mature tree.

We would also like to thank Jim Armstrong, the managing editor, for taking extraordinary care to help this project blossom.

We'd like to thank Mark Viquesney for reading early drafts of the manuscript and for his constructive criticism and suggestions. His friendship is invaluable.

We'd like to thank Ying's intern, Nicole Price, for her unparalleled diligence and organizational skills, making it possible for Ying to juggle multiple projects while finishing the last stages of this book.

Finally, we'd like to thank Greg, Ying's husband and Vinson's father, for his support and for calming the stormy seas that occasionally arose between us during the voyage of this project.

ILLUSTRATION CREDITS

Page 3: Courtesy Nanyang Technological University.

Page 6: Michael Coyne/National Geographic Creative.

Page 12: Courtesy Melissa Faulner.

Page 16: © Camphora/Wikimedia Commons, detail.

Page 27: Courtesy of the Society for Anglo-Chinese Understanding.

Page 32: Author's collection.

Page 38: Bruno Barbey/Magnum Photos.

Page 45: Scott S. Warren/National Geographic Creative.

Page 60: Jason Lee/Reuters Pictures.

Page 63: © Camphora/Wikimedia Commons.

Page 69: STR New/Reuters Pictures.

Page 81: ©iStockphoto.com/beemore.

Page 86: © Nniud/Dreamstime.com

Page 103: Courtesy Melissa Faulner.

Page 117: O. Louis Mazzatenta/National Geographic Creative.

Page 133: © Joe Kucharski/Dreamstime.com.

Page 169: © Vasily Pindyurin/123rf.com.

Page 171: O. Louis Mazzatenta/National Geographic Creative.

Page 185: Courtesy Cultural-China.com.

Page 191: © Su Jin Yan

Pages 203, 206, and 208: Author's collection.

ABOUT THE AUTHORS

YING CHANG COMPESTINE grew up during Mao's rule over China. Her young adult novel *Revolution Is Not a Dinner Party* was a critical success, won multiple awards, and was named by the American Library Association as a Best Book for Young Adults. In addition to her work as a writer, Ying visits schools throughout the United States and abroad, speaking about her journey as an author, how her life in China inspired her writing, and the challenges of writing in her second language. She lives in the East Bay, California. You can visit her at www.yingc.com.

Her son, **VINSON COMPESTINE,** was a National Merit Scholar and is currently studying at the University of Southern California's Marshall School of Business.

This book was designed by Maria T. Middleton. The text is set in 12-point Archer Light, a geometric slab-serif created by the Hoefler & Frere-Jones type foundry for *Martha Stewart Living* magazine in 2001. The display fonts are Triplex Sans and Stymie Extrabold Condensed.

This book was printed and bound by Worzalla in Stevens Point, Wisconsin. Its production was overseen by Kathy Lovisolo.